Murder at the Rose ❧

Murder at the Rose

An Elizabethan Mystery

by

Robert Gorrell

The Black Rock Press
University of Nevada, Reno
2000

Printed in the United States of America

ISBN 1-891033-17-4

The Black Rock Press
University Library/322
University of Nevada, Reno
Reno, NV 89557-0044

Cover illustrations courtesy the Folger Shakespeare Library.

Acknowledgements

I am grateful to Mike and Barbara Land, Joe Crowley, and my son Mark Gorrell for helpful comments on the manuscript, to Bob Blesse and the Black Rock Press for imaginative design, and to my wife Joie for everything.

Cast of Characters

Wat Gayton, a young beginning actor
Nell Simpkin, his landlady, a widow
Captain Bill Daglish, retired from the navy
Anne Page, friend of Wat
Philip Henslowe, manager of the Admiral's Men
Members of the Admiral's Men
  Edward Alleyn
  John Singer
  Thomas Towne
  Ed Juby
  Martin Slater
  Ed Tobye
  Thomas Hearne
  John Pig, Will Barne, boy actors for women's roles
Members of the Chamberlain's Men
  Richard Burbage
  Will Kempe
  William Shakespeare
  Thomas Pope
  John Heminges
Joan Alleyn, wife of Edward Alleyn, friend of Anne
John Page, vintner, father of Anne
Constable Philip Slocum, head of the watch
Elizabeth I, Queen of England
Robert Devereux, Earl of Essex
Elizabeth Brydges, one of the Queen's waiting women
Will Carlin, agent for the Queen's Council
Robert Cecil, adviser to the Queen
Richard Topcliffe, hunter of papists
Richard Skevington, Thomas Fowler, Topcliffe's men

Contents

1. A Broken Head   1
2. A New Play and Wat's first Role   9
3. Loud Words in High Places   19
4. "Much Virtue There Is in a Pot of Good Ale," Johnny Pig's Song   25
5. A Shot in the Last Act   31
6. The Return of Tobye   39
7. A Queen's Council Agent   49
8. Reappearance of a Pistol   57
9. A Scene Missing from a Shakespeare Play   65
10. A Masked Lady   71
11. "The Count of Exeter's Daughter Knows How To find Truth"   79
12. A Taste of the Rack and a Rescue   85
13. A Lesson in Love   93
14. A Girl and An Ambush   99
15. Old Armor Doesn't Bite   105
16. Fabrications and Skepticism   111
17. A Confrontation at the Theatre   117
18. A Different Elizabeth   125
19. Suspects in the Theatre   131
20. Carlin's Trap   135
21. A Riot at the Rose   141

Historical Note

ALTHOUGH THIS STORY is fictional, many of the characters are based on persons who were alive and busy in Elizabethan England, and many of the incidents actually occurred. Queen Elizabeth I and the Earl of Essex were quarreling and making up in 1597, as they often were. Elizabeth was sixty-four, and had been queen for thirty-nine years. Robert Dudley, later Earl of Leicester, who had been closest to Elizabeth in her earlier years on the throne, linked with her romantically in court gossip, had died in 1588. Essex, young, handsome, brash, often reckless, gradually took the place of Leicester in the Queen's affections. In 1597 he was achieving the popularity that later tempted him to open rebellion and disaster. William Cecil, Lord Burghley, was ill and reaching the end of his long service as Elizabeth's most trusted adviser, and his son Robert Cecil was rising in favor and influence.

Richard Topcliffe was out of prison in 1597, enjoying the Fitzherberts' house in Padley that he had appropriated and continuing his persecution of Roman Catholics. He had hounded the poet Robert Southwell, supervising his torture and collecting evidence that led to his execution in 1595. Unlike the character in the story, Topcliffe lived until 1604.

Philip Henslowe was manager of the Admiral's Men, and his account book or diary is one of the most significant sources for information about the Elizabethan theatre. Plays mentioned in the novel were part of the company's repertoire in 1597, many of them lost. Most of the actors and playwrights who appear in the novel were mentioned in Henslowe's diary or in other contemporary accounts, famous ones like Richard Burbage and Edward Alleyn and Will Kempe and Ben Jonson and William Shakespeare and also less well known actors like John Pig and John Singer and Thomas Towne and Ed Tobye and William Slater. Most of the details about their lives are fictional.

William Shakespeare, thirty-three years old, had been in London for seven or eight years. He was already a sharer in the Chamberlain's company and a successful poet and playwright. His romantic narrative poems had been successful, and he had served his apprenticeship as a writer for the theatre, learning from the popularity of chronicle plays, revenge tragedy, and Latin-based comedies. *Titus Andronicus* was still around, popular for its blood and thunder. *Henry VI* and *Richard II* and *Richard III* were on the stage, as were four or five early comedies, including *Love's Labour's Lost, Comedy of Errors,* and *Two Gentlemen of Verona.* Shakespeare had achieved some standing by 1597.

In the years that followed, before his death in 1616, he was to write the greatest plays in the English language. Ben Jonson, after his stint in Marshalsea prison in 1597 and a duel with Gabriel Spencer in 1598, concentrated on writing rather than acting. He perhaps ranks next to Shakespeare among the many significant dramatists of the period, with plays like *Volpone* and *The Alchemist.* The Chamberlain's Men became the King's Men in 1603, and Richard Burbage continued to lead the company until his death in 1619. Philip Henslowe became increasingly important in theatre management. He and his son-in-law Edward Alleyn built the Fortune playhouse in 1600, with Alleyn as the leading actor until he retired from the stage about 1606. Both Henslowe and Alleyn gained wealth from their theatrical enterprises, and Alleyn endowed a school and hospital in 1613, when he retired to his country estate. Henslowe died in 1616, Alleyn in 1626. *The Spanish Tragedy,* Henslowe's *Jeronimo,* continued for many years to appeal to the Elizabethan taste for blood and thunder, with revivals on the stage and nine printed editions, the latest in 1633. Nothing is known of Alleyn's apprentice, John Pig, after an appearance at the Rose about 1599. Will Kempe in 1600 performed a Morris dance from London to Norwich, described in his book, *Kemps Nine Daies Wonder.*

The records of the London Commissioner of the Sewers refer in 1606 to the Rose as "the late playhouse." The theatre had apparently been torn down or converted to other uses, and like other Elizabethan playhouses was only a memory. But in 1989 construction crews unearthed the foundations of the old building, and a vigorous campaign by the elite of England's acting professon stopped the bulldozers from clearing away the stones. The foundations were preserved, even though an office building was erected over them, and in 1999 a damp basement was opened to visitors who can view the remains of the Rose.

O monstrous resolution of a wretch
See, Viceroy, he hath bitten forth his tongue,
Rather than to reveal what we required.

—Thomas Kyd, *The Spanish Tragedy*

For murder, though it have no tongue, will speak
With most miraculous organ.

—William Shakespeare, *Hamlet*

Chapter One

❦

A Broken Head

WAT GAYTON woke early on his seventeenth birthday. It was early April; there was still a hint of winter chill in the London air, but the sun was already showing. Wat was happy, looking forward to a good day.

Mrs. Simpkin, in whose house he had a room, was already up.

"Marry, Wat, you're slow today," she called, "Come now, if you'd be eating. The Captain's already at table."

There was water in the pitcher beside Wat's bed. He splashed some on his face, pulled on hose and doublet, and joined the widow Simpkin and his fellow-boarder in front of the kitchen fire.

Nell Simpkin was a large plump woman, well into her forties, but still able to attract leers from the Thames boatmen. She announced frequently that she would be a slave to no man; she mothered Wat and browbeat the Captain, her other boarder. She ladled porridge into a bowl.

"You need something to stick to your ribs on a day like this. Happy Birthday, young Wat."

Wat thanked her and joined the Captain at the table.

Mrs. Simpkin had been making a scanty living for fifteen years by renting two rooms in the house and doing a variety of sewing jobs. Her husband John Simpkin at twenty had been the youngest member of the local watch. The other two and the ancient constable had learned to stay away from any violence; but John was conscientious and eager, and he undertook the single-handed arrest of a pickpocket outside the Curtain theatre. He was fatally stabbed, the thief escaped, and Nell Simpkin became the widow

Simpkin. She blamed the Curtain and the theatres, convinced that wickedness infested them all.

Captain Bill Daglish was nearly sixty, with a frizzled gray beard and a patch over his left eye. He had been a fixture in the house ever since the widow had started taking in boarders. He had a small pension, which financed his leisurely existence and presumably attested to the military career responsible for his title. He spoke often of his valor in exploits against the savage tribes of Ireland, and had ready advice for the efforts of the Earl of Essex and others in their attempts to subdue the island. He deplored the introduction of new weapons to replace the sword and buckler, but he wore a rapier, now more fashionable, and frequently threatened to draw it. Rumors in the neighborhood fashioned explicit details of a romance between the Captain and the widow, but there was little foundation for them. He sat on a joint stool, savoring his morning pint of ale.

"Well, Wat, my lad, and do you think you'll make a man before your sister?" It was the Captain's standard greeting, and Wat had learned that no reply was expected. "How will you be spending your birthday?"

"I'm off to the Rose. I can get a few pence taking care of horses, and Mr. Henslowe has promised to think about giving me a try on the stage—what I've been hoping for all these months."

"Good luck to you, lad. But keep an eye out on your way this morning. Rogues get out early."

The London Wat was hoping to conquer, population perhaps 150,000, was partly an overgrown village, partly a busy metropolis. The City, north of the Thames, was a crowded commercial district, but outside there were still remnants of country estates. Streets were narrow, some cobbled but some only mud tracks that became hazards for coachmen in rough weather. Buildings were crowded together. Garbage disposal was negligible; chamber pots were often emptied out of windows. Kites, long-winged and sharp-beaked, flourished in the city in great numbers because of the lavish supply of refuse for scavenging, including the heads of erstwhile traitors on spikes near the law courts. The city was infested with rogues and vagabonds of all sorts—cut-purses, cony-catchers, cross-biters, shifters, foists, and other con artists. Robert Greene, playwright, novelist, and pamphleteer, wrote about the London underworld and commented that an excellent foist or pickpocket "must have three properties that a good surgeon should have, and that is an Eagles eie to spy a purchase, to have a quick insight where the boung [purse] lies, and then a Lyon's heart not to feare what the end will bee, and then a Ladies hand to be little and nimble, the better to dive into the pocket." In spite of the readiness of juries to hang any thieves who were caught, the laws and the courts seemed always behind the ingenuity of the London underworld.

People were already stirring as Wat walked along the Thames, the main thoroughfare of the city. A costermonger, whom Wat saw nearly every morning waved cordially. A fishmonger, also up early, called out "Whiting, fresh whiting." One peddler was calling "rock samphires," selling one of the chief condiments of the time, which grew on the rocky cliffs near the sea and was used as a pickle or put fresh into salads. Wat walked past the Bear Garden, already noisy with the sounds of the dogs, who would be busy later in the day nipping at Old Sackerson or some other popular bear. The one time Wat and the Captain had attended a bear-baiting, Wat found himself siding with the bear.

The Rose, built ten years earlier by Philip Henslowe, who also owned the Bear Garden, had become the most popular theatre in London, located on the Bankside, near the river, easily accessible from the main parts of the city. Unlike the octagonal Bear Garden, the Rose was circular, finished on the outside with lath and plaster, with a stage, a yard, galleries, a tiring house, and a flagpole. Henslowe had spent 108 pounds in 1595 on renovations, adding seven pounds a little later for "making the throne in the heavens." The theatre was attractive.

The Rose and the Bear Garden on the Bankside, as well as the stews and gambling houses, were important for the watermen, who ferried patrons across the Thames. Officials and owners of the great houses along the river had private barges, but there were also many wherries for hire at public stairs. John Taylor, who called himself the Water Poet and wrote extensively of the "noble Thames," estimated that there were two thousand small boats about London. Watermen seemed always available, shouting "Westward Ho!" or "Eastward Ho!"

The old Theatre, the first playhouse in London, built in 1576, and the Curtain, north of the city near Finsbury Fields, were still active. They housed the Chamberlain's Men, the company headed by Richard Burbage and including Thomas Pope, John Heminges, William Shakespeare, and comedian Will Kempe They had been producing early plays of Shakespeare and Ben Jonson and were successful.

Philip Henslowe, however, with a stable of writers producing a steady stream of new plays, had the most active program. In 1597 there were at least seven new plays at the Rose. The company, the Admiral's Men, was headed by Edward Alleyn, Henslowe's son-in-law, and included John Singer, John Pig, Thomas Towne, Martin Slater, Thomas Downton, Ed Juby, and James Donstone. Wat was hoping for a minor role in George Chapman's comedy *An Humorous Day's Mirth*, scheduled to open in a day or two. The company had great hopes for the play, capitalizing on the current fad for plays with "humorous" characters—characters, often comic, with an excess of one of the four bodily humors, blood or phlegm or black or yellow bile. The Chamberlain's Men at the Curtain were rehearsing *Every Man in his Humor*, a new play by Ben Jonson, with the same humors theme and with characters named to suggest their controlling traits—Brainworm, Wellbred, Formal, Downright. Henslowe, who was not a scholar, noted them in his account book as comedies of "umers." Wat had too much beard and too deep a voice to qualify for one of the women's roles, but there were other parts he hoped for.

Wat could see the Rose as he passed the Bear Garden, with its flag already signaling that there'd be a performance. The entrance in the front to the yard was locked; he walked around to the tiring house door. It was ajar; workmen had apparently come in early to prepare for the afternoon performance. But Wat heard no sounds of activity. He walked through the dressing rooms and looked out into the yard; it was deserted. He turned to the stage. Someone was seated on a chair in the corner. Wat called, but got no answer. He walked over to a figure slumped forward on the chair, and in the dim light got a closer look at what was left of his head. Wat had never seen a dead person, but there was no doubt about this. He ran over to the edge of the stage and vomited.

Wat had recognized the dead man, Timothy Rudd, well-known around the theatre, a kind of handy man kept in sack and in debt by Henslowe, helpful with the stage machinery during performances and able occasionally to fill in a bit part. He was no longer young; the blood was shiny on his gray hair.

Wat went back into the tiring house and called for help, but nobody answered. He went out into the street and called out for the watch. No officer seemed to be about, but passersby picked up the cry, and Wat was soon listening to loud questions and trying to explain what had happened. The crowd followed him back into the theatre.

"He's dead all right," said a waterman who was stopping on his way down to his boat on the river. "It's old Timothy. He never hurt anyone."

"He won't hurt anyone now," said another.

They stared discreetly at what remained of Timothy Rudd, imagining the violence of the blows that had shattered his head.

The noise finally roused someone on the watch, and Constable Philip Slocum came into the theatre. Slocum was tall and heavy, with broad shoulders and big hands. He had a curly brown beard, and a scowl that could make him look ominous. The group on the stage moved back to give him a view of the corpse.

"He's dead," Slocum announced. "Who did this?"

There was no answer. He surveyed the crowd that was growing as people outside realized that something had happened. Someone walked over to get a closer view of a bloody axe lying near the corpse.

Slocum hurried toward him, gesturing excitedly. "Stand back there. Nobody touch anything."

Slocum had been told to say this at the scene of a crime. It was his first experience with murder. He then violated his order and picked up the axe. "Who owns this?"

Again there was no answer. Slocum assumed his most professional manner. "This is a serious matter. It looks like murder to me, and I'd better start getting some answers."

"That axe came from the work room in the theatre," somebody said.

Slocum turned. "Who are you? And what do you know about the axe?"

"I've been working back stage this morning. I saw that axe. Somebody left it on the stage."

Slocum accepted his answer; then turned and looked sternly at the crowd.

"Who found him?"

Wat stepped forward. "He was like this when I came in just a few minutes ago."

"Was there anybody else around?"

"I didn't see anybody. I called for help, but nobody answered, so I went outside to look for the watch."

"The old man wouldn't have tempted a robber," said Slocum. He turned to Wat. "What did you have against him? And what's your name and what are you doing here?"

"I'm Wat Gayton. I help around the theatre. I came to see Mr. Henslowe."

"Does anybody here know this boy?"

There was silence, and then a man moved up from the back of the crowd. "I know him," he said. "He works for Henslowe, more fool he."

Wat and most of the crowd recognized the newcomer as the most famous clown on the London stage.

"Are you Will Kempe?" asked Slocum.

The man did a little dance. "Cavaliero Kempe, headmaster of Morrice dancers, and one of the Chamberlain's Men," he said.

Wat had no idea why Kempe should speak for him. He had seen him playing Peter in *Romeo and Juliet* at the Curtain, but he was sure that Kempe had never even been aware of the existence of Wat Gayton.

"The boy wouldn't have had anything to do with this," said Kempe. "And old Timothy's not much of a loss. He'd make good eating for the kites, but he's probably so full of sack he'd make 'em drunk." His try for a joke was not a success.

"What are you doing here, Will Kempe?" Another voice came from the back of the crowd, and Philip Henslowe became the center of attention.

"Afraid I'll steal your audience, Henslowe? I'm not looking for a job. And this is a scurvy trick for trying to fill your house." Kempe motioned toward the corpse.

"You've no business here, Kempe."

"What did old Rudd find out? Is somebody pirating plays. Or was he just going to expose the tear-throat acting in the Rose?"

"You go back and talk to Dick Burbage about tear-throat acting. And while you're at it, you might ask him whether that play about Richard II is really treasonous. There's talk around."

Slocum stepped between the two. "We've got a murder here, and I've got my duty to do."

He turned to Wat again. "That looks like blood on your shoe."

Wat had stepped into the puddle of blood near the victim when he walked up to him.

"You're coming with me," Slocum said.

"There's no need to take the boy," Henslowe stepped between Wat and Slocum. "He had nothing to do with this."

"It's right he should be questioned," Slocum said. "I know my duty." He turned to Henslowe. "And for you it's best to get the old man out of here and buried and to get this mess cleaned up."

He pushed Wat ahead of him and they left. It was Slocum's greatest moment as an officer of the law.

Chapter Two

❦

A New Play and Wat's First Role

A NNE PAGE had long yellow hair and bright blue eyes. She was slim, of medium height. Her mouth seemed always about to break into a smile, but it seldom did. She was wearing a simple long gray skirt and a blue laced doublet, without the puffed sleeves or heavy farthingale affected by ladies of fashion. Anne's father, John Page, was a successful vintner, proprietor of the Mitre tavern. Her mother was a long-time friend of Mrs. Simpkin, who sewed for her, and Anne often carried messages or presents of food to the widow's house. Wat had met her soon after his arrival in London. He had learned when she was likely to pay a visit, and he often made himself available to walk home with her.

Anne learned about the murder, overhearing the talk of the players who came into the Mitre. She had never allowed herself to think much about Wat. But she was vaguely aware that she was finding more excuses for visiting the widow Simpkin, and that she was disappointed if Wat didn't appear to walk home with her. She was concerned when she learned that Wat had been hauled off to Marshalsea prison by the watch, although she wasn't quite sure why. She slipped off at once to find her friend Joan Alleyn, wife of the famous actor at the Rose and stepdaughter of Henslowe, the manager.

Actors didn't have much influence in London affairs, but Edward Alleyn was not only an actor, he was a partner in Philip Henslowe's enterprises and was respected as a business man. He knew Wat and was considering trying him in a part in the new George Chapman humors play soon to open at the Rose.

He knew about the murder and Wat's arrest before Anne and Joan came to ask for help. He set off at once for the Marshalsea. He had no trouble convincing Slocum and some other members of the watch that Wat was innocent.

Wat had grown up in the small town of Tunbridge, about twenty miles southeast of London, the youngest of three children. His father was a modestly successful stationer, respected in the community, a church warden. His mother had Irish ancestors, who were probably responsible for Wat's reddish blonde hair and blue-green eyes. Although both parents faithfully attended the Church of England parish church, where Wat learned his catechism from Cranmer's prayer book, Wat's mother, with relatives still in Ireland, had some sympathy for the Catholic clergy, like the poet Robert Southwell, who had been persecuted under the new harsh laws and hanged in 1595.

Wat had entered the Tunbridge grammar school at the age of six, learning his letters from a hornbook, learning to read and write from a primer and copy book, and then turning to William Lily's famous Latin grammar, which he practically memorized, encouraged by frequent applications of the schoolmaster's rod. He had for ten years been in school from seven in the morning to five in the afternoon, with time to go home for a noon meal. He had worked through the Latin of Aesop's Fables and Virgil's Eclogues without enthusiasm, but had found some excitement in Ovid and then had found his real interest when he came to the Roman playwrights, Terence and especially Plautus. He played the noble soldier in a school production of Plautus's *Miles Gloriosus*. When he was sixteen, he was happy to escape the rigid discipline of school. He had developed a strong romantic enthusiasm for what he imagined as the London theatre. When a traveling company passed through Tunbridge playing the old chestnut *Cambises*, Wat determined to take the few shillings he had saved from odd jobs and try his luck in London.

Wat didn't quite know what to say when he found Anne waiting with Joan Alleyn at the theatre. He had known many of the girls in the village, even kissed a few of them on May Day, but his feelings for Anne were new to him.

"I'm glad to find you safe," Anne said.

Wat was embarrassed. "My thanks to all of you," he said; and then, as quickly as he could without seeming impolite, he turned to Anne, "May I walk home with you?"

They walked toward the Mitre. "It must have been a shock," Anne said, "coming on old Timothy like that. Were you afraid?"

"Not much."

"Had you ever seen a dead man before?"

"No, but I knew he was dead."

They were silent for several minutes, but Wat took Anne's hand. Anne changed the subject.

"Joan says that Henslowe's going to give you a try in the new play."

"I hope so." Wat suddenly realized that it was getting late. "If he's thinking of that, I'd better be getting back before any rehearsals begin."

Wat left her at the entrance to the Mitre and hurried back to the Rose. The actors were gathering, and Alleyn was distributing parts for the new play. He came to Wat, who was standing behind the regular members of the company.

"How would you like to try the role of Jacques, Verone's man? It's not a big part, but it's important. Do you think you can learn it?"

"I'm sure I can. I'll have the lines tomorrow."

Wat was excited and eager. They ran through the play, using the written parts and trying to deal with the elaborate puns that made up much of the dialogue. Wat read his lines clearly, and the others seemed to accept him.

The next few days were busy, and Wat almost forgot old Timothy and the murder. The company was busy rehearsing for the opening of the new humors play but also doing performances nearly every day of plays from their repertoire, the popular *French Comedy, Alexander and Lodowick*, and others.

Alleyn found no role in the new Chapman comedy that interested him. He had made his reputation as Tamburlaine the Great in Marlowe's play or as Barabas in *The Jew of Malta* and was best in majestic characterizations. He was tall, more than six feet, with a dark curly beard. The players called him Mr. Alleyn. He took the part of the King in the humors play, although it was not a dominating role.

Wat was especially interested in John Singer, who was developing a reputation as a comic actor and was assigned the role of Lemot in Chapman's new play. Singer was thin, with a sharp nose and pointed chin, and Wat admired his sophisticated management of Chapman's elaborate puns, playing in one scene on Lemot's name as French for "the word," confusing it with *mote* and *moat* and *mought* for a dozen lines.

"They're some of the worst puns in the English or French language," Singer commented to Wat, "but the groundlings think they're funny."

Singer suggested to Wat a different way of reading some of his lines, putting more stress on the ends of sentences. He seemed friendly, and Wat was grateful and flattered by the attention.

Wat was not much older than the boys who were playing the female roles in the play, and he quickly became friends with John Pig, playing the Countess, and Will Barne, playing Florila. Pig had been pulled from his school in London by a recruiter for the children's company of St. Paul's chapel and had shown promise in his first play. But he resisted the strict religious discipline of the master of the children and ran away after a couple of months. He somehow came to the notice of Edward Alleyn, who supported his refusal to return and took him as his apprentice. He had been with Alleyn for three or four years and was nearly Wat's age. Barne, referred to as "little Will," was less experienced, but he was playing three or four important women's parts.

There was not much time for anything but serious work as the company got the Chapman play ready for its May 11 opening, and Wat was surprised when Thomas Towne, one of the sharers in the company, came up to him during a break in the rehearsal.

"What do you hear about old Timothy's murder?" he asked.

"Nothing," Wat answered. "Has something happened?"

Towne and Singer had both been members of the Admiral's company since 1594, and Singer had been playing in London for ten years before that, mainly with the Queen's Men. Along with Alleyn they had had many of the most important roles in the Admiral's repertory. They, especially Towne, had shown more interest in the murder than most of the company. Wat thought they might have heard something new.

"Didn't you get questioned by the man from the Queen's Council who was around yesterday?"

Towne liked to impress the company with his knowledge of London politics. He boasted of friends at court, especially among members of the Queen's Council, who were interested in the theatres and alert to discover any seditious material in the plays or any questionable behavior in the actors. In the new play he had the role of Count Labervele, a jealous and gullible husband. Wat didn't like Towne much, but he recognized his prestige in the company, and he was impressed by references to the Queen's Council.

"Nobody asked me anything," he assured Towne.

"You'd better be thinking about some answers." Towne's manner suggested that he had some kind of special information. "The Council wants to know what really happened with old Timothy's murder."

"I told the watch all I know," Wat said.

"The Council agent thinks the old man found out some-thing and had to be silenced. You remember Will Kempe suggested that. He'll want to know what you were doing in the theatre that early in the morning."

"I always come in that early."

"Well, if you're covering for somebody, you'd better think again." Towne walked off. Wat wondered what he was talking about.

He saw John Pig near the back tiring house stairs trying on a new gown. Henslowe had paid the tailor more than twenty shillings for taffeta and tinsel to make new gowns for the play, and Pig was checking his new costume.

"Have you heard any talk about a Queen's Council man asking about old Timothy?" Wat asked.

Pig was silent for a minute and looked a little embarrassed. "I'm not supposed to talk about it."

Pig, as Alleyn's apprentice and a favorite of Joan Alleyn, was in a position to hear a good deal of the talk among the veteran actors.

"Are they thinking I had something to do with the murder? Does Mr. Alleyn think so?"

"Oh, no," Pig said, but Wat was worried. He went back to studying his lines, but he kept trying to remember whether he had seen or heard anything that morning when he had found old Tim with his head smashed. He knew that the Constable thought the murder had occurred during the night, and he knew Mrs. Simpkin and the Captain could swear that he had been at home that night.

But he was not surprised when later in the morning Edward Alleyn called him and said that an investigator from the Queen's Council was in Mr. Henslowe's room and wanted to talk with him.

"There's nothing to worry about," he assured Wat, but Wat was not sure. He had heard stories about the rack and the thumbscrew, and even in Tunbridge he had heard about Council men looking for traitors. As a boy he had heard stories about plots against the Queen during the past dozen years and the fate of various traitors. Some of the grown-ups in Tunbridge had heard bells and seen bonfires and dancing in the streets of London when Anthony Babington and others had been arrested for their roles in an awkward plot to kill the Queen, allegedly with the support of Mary, Queen of Scots. Babington and six of his confederates were paraded through the city to St. Giles Fields and hanged, drawn, and quartered, as a warning to all would-be traitors. A few citizens had made the journey from Tunbridge to witness the execution of Mary, and liked to tell about the wig slipping from her severed head, revealing her gray hair. Some of his neighbors in Tunbridge were vigorous supporters of Peter Wentworth and other Puritan reformers, who defied Queen Elizabeth's messages forbidding religious discussions in Parliament. Wentworth, after a sojourn in the Tower, remained a leader of the Puritan movement until his death in 1596.

Wat had been too absorbed in school and his interest in the theatre to pay much attention to such events. He had heard some political talk around the Rose, and John Pig sometimes hinted about gossip he heard in Alleyn's house. But Wat was almost totally innocent and naive in matters of religion and politics, and he was frightened of the unknown as he made his way to Henslowe's office.

The two officers from the Council seemed friendly, and Wat lost his nervousness as they questioned him about his background and family. He became concerned when one of them, called Will Carlin, asked him about a neighbor in Tunbridge.

"We hope you know your duty to the Queen and her Council and are ready to talk freely. Treason is a serious crime."

Wat had no trouble agreeing.

Then Carlin launched on a series of quick questions about Tunbridge: "Do you know one James Coburn? Is he a Puritan? Have you ever heard him say anything disloyal to the Queen? Do you know that he was a friend of Peter Wentworth, who spent time in the Tower because of his slanders?"

Wat was completely confused. He remembered James Coburn and had heard him talk about hunting deer and drinking ale, but nothing about religion or the Queen. He stammered answers.

Then Carlin took another approach. "What Catholics do you know in Tunbridge?"

Wat couldn't think of any.

"Didn't your mother's family come from Ireland? Weren't they Catholic?"

"I guess so," Wat said. "But we're all Church of England. My father's a warden in the parish church."

Then Carlin turned to the murder of old Timothy, and Wat had to describe his morning in the theatre again, professing his ignorance of any wrongdoing that the old man might have uncovered. And then:

"How well do you know the player called Thomas Towne?"

"He's a shareholder in the company I know."

"You were seen talking to him yesterday. What did you talk about?"

"We talked about the new play. I have a part in it. It's my first regular part."

"What did he say about old Timothy and the murder?"

"He just asked if I'd been questioned. And he told me you were here."

There was silence for a minute or two, and then the officer turned to Wat with an intensity that was almost ominous.

"What have you heard Towne say concerning the Earl of Essex?"

Wat was surprised. He had, of course, heard of Essex as an important favorite of the Queen and a successful leader. And Johnny Pig had hinted that the Chamberlain's Men might have some trouble about Essex. Towne, however, had never talked to him about Essex. The officer accepted his denial.

"How about Ed Tobye? Has he talked about Essex?"

"I hardly know Tobye," Wat said.

"If you do hear any talk about Essex, you're to let me know."

The officer went back to the morning of the murder.

"What's your relationship with the player Will Kempe?"

"I've seen him perform. He's very funny."

"Why did he vouch for you on the morning when you discovered the body?"

"I don't know," said Wat. "He must have heard who I was from Mr. Alleyn."

"What are you covering up? What was Kempe doing in the Rose at that hour?"

Wat's confusion was probably so obvious that the officers believed him. They dismissed him, but with a warning that he was to report anything he heard around the playhouse concerning Essex or the players he had mentioned.

Wat went back to the rehearsal, trying to sort out what he had been hearing. He thought over again his discovery of the body of old Timothy, wondering whether he had overlooked important details. He wondered what the Earl of Essex could have to do with players at the Rose. He tried to think of reasons for Will Kempe's appearance and his support. He thought again of his conversation with Thomas Towne. And Towne was waiting for him.

"What did you tell the officers?" he asked. "Did they ask about me?"

"They asked what we talked about yesterday. I just told them you asked me if I'd been questioned."

"You better watch yourself," Towne said and walked off.

Chapter Three

❦

Loud Words in High Places

JUST A FEW DAYS before Wat Gayton's birthday and his first chance at a role in a London play, there were loud words in the private quarters of Queen Elizabeth. Robert Devereux, Earl of Essex, was pleading with the Queen for a special favor on behalf of a friend, Sir Robert Sidney. He was urging the appointment of Sidney to the Wardenship of the Cinque Ports, a position vacated by the death of old Lord Cobham. Essex had no particular reason for his uncompromising enthusiasm for Sidney, except the fact that he hated the son of Cobham, the candidate favored by Lord Burghley and Elizabeth. Essex had begun with the kind of approach that had served him well in the past.

"Your gracious majesty, you know well my great love for you and my unwavering devotion to the future of your reign. I press this suit only in my duty to your greatness."

"I think you know of my disposition in this case, to favor the young Lord Cobham."

"Favor me no favors! I must have the Wardenship for Sidney."

"Headstrong and intemperate," Elizabeth almost shouted. "Do you question the wisdom or the authority of the Queen?"

"I will spend all my might and influence to procure it for him. And I will abide no other decision."

"The matter is decided." Elizabeth left the room.

Essex stormed out, shouting that he was leaving to visit his estate in Wales.

Elizabeth commented to Burghley in the next room. "I shall break him of his will, and pull down this o'erweening ambition, which comes from his mother." The Queen was referring to Lettice

Knowles, the widow of the Earl of Leicester. Leicester had preceded Essex as the Queen's favorite.

Essex sulked for a week and then prepared to carry out his threat and ride off into the country. Men and horses were ready to depart when Elizabeth sent for him.

"Most fair, most dear, and most excellent Sovereign," Essex began, as he apologized for his tantrum a week earlier. "I beg you to remember my past devotion and forgive my intemperance."

Elizabeth, as she often had before, forgave. Then in a gesture to save face for Essex and restore him to favor, she made him Master of the Ordnance, an office that he had earlier shunned as too insignificant for his talents.

Essex had achieved the height of his popularity. He had led a variety of naval and military exploits, with more flair than wisdom, but had acquired a following of hundreds of young men eager for adventure and attracted by prospects of looting. The dispute with Elizabeth over the Sidney appointment was typical of their stormy relationship, and the subsequent reconciliation indicated the durability of Elizabeth's attachment. She recognized the value of Essex's services and was moved by his flattery, but she also recognized the danger of his increasing popularity, tempting his followers, and sometimes Essex himself, always to seek more power. Essex, though still genuinely devoted, was more and more aware that Elizabeth, in spite of her wit and quick mind, was aging rapidly in looks. She was sixty-four years old in 1597 and had been queen for thirty-nine years. As an ambassador wrote, her face was long and thin, capped by a large reddish-colored wig, and her teeth, always irregular, had gone yellow.

Elizabeth was increasingly concerned about the security of the throne. She had dealt with a variety of plots, both real and imaginary, against the throne and her life. The person willingly or unwillingly implicated in many of the plots, Mary of Scotland, had been executed in 1587. The pressures on her to marry and provide a successor to the throne had pretty much disappeared after the death in 1584 of the Duke of Alençon, the last and most persistent of her suitors. She was, however, irritated by intrigue among her courtiers and her ladies in waiting. Sir Walter Ralegh, for example, an earlier favorite of the Queen, had had an affair with Elizabeth Throgmorton, one of the Queen's ladies in waiting. When the Queen, who thought of herself as a kind of parent to her ladies, learned that Throgmorton was pregnant, Ralegh went to the Tower, and after his release was forbidden to appear in court. He never regained complete favor, although he acquired popular support from his participation with Essex in expeditions against the Spanish in 1596.

Elizabeth relied heavily on William Cecil, Lord Burghley, who had been the most trusted and influential statesman in the court since Elizabeth first took the throne. Burghley was an old man in 1597, but he had groomed his youngest son, Robert Cecil, to succeed him. Robert had inherited his father's intelligence and aptitude for statesmanship, but he had been a sickly child, and he grew up small and humpbacked. Elizabeth called him her pigmy, but she came to trust him and appointed him Secretary in 1596. The Queen relied on him to deal with the rumors of plots and treasons constantly plaguing the court. He also attempted to be a deterrent to the ambitions of Essex.

Essex had become a favorite of the Queen at about the time of the defeat of the Spanish Armada in 1588. He became especially important to Elizabeth after the death of Robert Dudley, Earl of Leicester, the same year. Lord Burghley was not a supporter of Essex, but the handsome young courtier's exploits kept him in the Queen's and the public's eye.

For example, three years before the dispute over Sidney's appointment, Essex had discovered what he called a "most dangerous and desperate treason" involving the Queen's physician, a Portuguese Jew named Lopez. Elizabeth assigned old Burghley and son Robert to examine Lopez. They found nothing to substantiate Essex's charges. There was another scene in the Queen's private quarters.

"You are a rash and temerarious youth to enter into a matter against the poor man which you can not prove."

Essex rushed away in anger but, unfortunately for Lopez, considered it a matter of honor to validate his charges. He found dubious evidence of a poison plot; Lopez was tried and convicted. Elizabeth was not convinced of his guilt and ordered his execution postponed, but Essex somehow circumvented the order. Lopez was hanged before a large cheering audience and, according to legal routine, cut down still alive and castrated, disemboweled, and quartered. Again Essex's popularity increased, and later he was able to charm his way back into Elizabeth's favor.

He rose still higher in the popular mind in 1596 with the famous exploit of Essex and Admiral Thomas Howard and Sir Walter Ralegh against Cadiz. In spite of constant rivalry over command and a variety of mistakes, Cadiz was burned and plundered, and Essex returned triumphant and glorious, having again cemented relations with his followers with generous distributions of booty and a number of knighthoods. Elizabeth, however, remembered that she had authorized £50,000 to finance the expedition and that forty richly-laden Spanish ships had been burned by their commanders while the English concentrated on looting the town. The estimated booty returned to the crown was less than £13,000, and Elizabeth was not pleased.

About the time Henslowe's men were preparing for the first performance of the Chapman humors play, however, a different sort of scene was being played in the Queen's private quarters. After a series of quarrels earlier in the summer, Essex and Elizabeth were basking in an air of reconciliation.

"I humbly kiss your royal fair hands," Essex had written, "and pour out my soul in passionate jealous wishes for all true joys to the dear heart of your Majesty."

Elizabeth had sent gifts and put Essex in charge of the fleet to be dispatched for another venture against the Spanish, who were supposedly preparing another armada. She wished him success, and urged him to be careful of his own life.

"I have heard that your ship has leaks," she warned. "You must take precautions for your safety."

Essex was at his most effusive: "Heavens and earth shall witness for me. I will strive to be worthy of so high a grace and so blessed a happiness."

The farewell concluded in complete harmony. The Queen was in her most benign mood, partly because she was still savoring her triumph in an encounter with an ambassador from the King of Poland. The ambassador had been invited for a public audience. He appeared and kissed the Queen's hand, and then immediately launched into a tirade in Latin, neg-lecting all the usual diplomatic courtesies for a series of threats and warnings. Elizabeth rose from her throne and in extempore Latin chastised him soundly for his insolence and audacity. The court was delighted with her performance, and Essex, who heard the story from Cecil, told her that she "was made of the same stuff of which the ancients believed the heroes to be formed; that is, her mind of gold, her body of brass."

Even Burghley and Cecil were sharing in the tranquility around the court, reconciled to Essex and supporting his expedition. Robert Cecil, however, and the Privy Council remained constantly alert to the dangers of threats to the throne. Cecil viewed with some trepidation the continuing surge of popular feeling for Essex, which Essex had done nothing to discourage. Soldiers who had served under him remained fiercely loyal, especially because of his generous distribution of spoils after a victory. Essex had also knighted large numbers of his leaders after battles. Robert Cecil, who had taken over most of the duties of his ailing father, heeded Elizabeth's charge that he be vigilant in exposing treason and sedition. Cecil did not tell her that the major concern of the Council was with followers of the Earl of Essex.

Cecil also was concerned with the growing influence of the theatres and the possibilities that actors were involved in movements dangerous to Queen. His agent Will Carlin had been assigned to investigate in the theatres, especially to look into the murder in the Rose. Cecil also knew about Elizabeth's displeasure with a play of the Chamberlain's Men in which a usurper deposes King Richard II. Elizabeth had been heard to say that she identified herself with Richard. And a man named Richard Topcliffe, whom Cecil remembered for his zeal in seeking out treason a year or two earlier, had warned the Council that a new play at the Swan needed to be investigated. Carlin was already busy, interested in the young actor who had found the body on the stage at the Rose and also in other players, especially Thomas Towne, Will Kempe, and John Singer. Will Carlin was ambitious to make a name for himself.

He would have been interested in Wat's early morning encounter the day after his interview with the young actor. Wat as usual turned up at the Rose early and entered at the main gate. He walked through the pit toward the stage; everything was quiet. And then with a feeling almost of panic he thought he saw again old Timothy Rudd. Someone was on his knees just where Wat had found the body. He heard Wat's step and stood.

"Good morning," he said. "You're young Wat, aren't you?"

Wat said "Good morning." He recognized Ed Tobye, one of the actors he had never talked to.

"This is where you found old Tim, isn't it? Have you remembered any more about it? Did you see anybody?"

"I talked to the watch. I don't know anything."

"Well, if you remember anything, I want to know. But you'd better not tell anybody about seeing me here."

Tobye walked off. Wat decided he wouldn't say anything about the meeting. He was tired of questions about the murder.

Chapter Four

❦

"Much Virtue There Is in a Pot of Good Ale," Johnny Pig's Song

CHAPMAN'S NEW PLAY was a great success. Wat was completely happy. He had played his small role enthusiastically and had drawn a few laughs from the groundlings. He watched Singer as Lemot, got a feel for his sense of timing and his ability to make the most of the lines, some of them difficult in Chapman's complex style. Alleyn and Henslowe both seemed pleased by his performance; and when the Admiral's Men opened another new play, *Frederick and Basilea*, on June 3, Wat had a small part. He thought of himself as a real actor and felt comfortable with other members of the company.

It was a busy summer. The Rose had a performance almost every day, and the players had to be ready to shift from one play to another as several different characters. *The Comedy of Humors* and *Frederick and Basilea* each had half a dozen performances in June, and Wat worked hard. Veterans like Alleyn were prepared in a dozen roles, some of them in revivals from earlier years. The Admiral's Men presented thirteen different plays in June, three of them new.

Henslowe's operation was successful as Elizabethan England continued to be merry England, with attendance at the theatres only one of a variety of amusements. People liked to sing, for example. Ballad mongers hawked their songs in the streets, tipplers sang in the taverns. More sophisticated music was common in many drawing rooms. A gentleman or lady could sight-read and sing a part in the complicated Elizabethan madrigals. Many could play on the virginals, the piano of the time, or the lute or the recorder. Enthusiasm in the singing as well as general noisy excitement was probably intensified because Elizabethans did not drink much water. Tea had not yet become the national drink; ale was the standard beverage, for breakfast and throughout the day. Almost everyone was perhaps slightly tipsy much of the time.

In spite of his busy schedule, Wat was finding more time for interests outside the theatre. With his new self-confidence, he was seeing more of Anne Page, both at her father's Mitre tavern and at Mrs. Simpkin's. They often went for walks into the fields north of London on days when there were no plays. On some Sundays there were country dances nearby, and Wat and Anne joined. Wat had played one of the dragons in a May Day morris dance in Tunbridge. Occasionally they went to one of the other theatres, especially the Curtain.

One afternoon when Wat was not acting, Anne took him across the river to Fleet Street, the show place of the town. Wat had never seen anything like the crowds of people or the variety of entertainment. They stopped to watch a puppet show, Punch with a long hooked nose and his shrewish wife Judy, with much beating and much name-calling. Another puppet show called itself *London and Ninevah* and attempted to warn Londoners that their immoral behavior could lead to a fate like that of Ninevah as described in the Bible. Acrobats entertained a crowd on one corner, jugglers on another.

Wat was fascinated by a ballad-monger, singing from a printed broadside that described an alleged miraculous birth of "The Two Inseparable Brothers," with a picture of a young man with a small twin attached to his breast. He noticed among the stack of other ballads being offered one called "Every Man in his Humour," which was the title of the new Jonson play the Chamberlain's Men were rehearsing. Another was titled "The Spanish Tragedy," which Wat realized referred to the *Jeronimo* play the Admiral's Men were reviving. The most popular exhibit offered a look for a penny at three naked Indians, who had been brought as curiosities from America. Wat and Anne went on to St. Paul's Cathedral at the end of Fleet Street and observed merchants and lawyers conducting business in the middle aisle, a general meeting place more than a place for worship.

Mrs. Simpkin was concerned about the behavior of Wat and Anne, and she occasionally quoted a Puritan preacher she had heard talking about "the noble science of heathen deviltry" or "the horrible vice of pestiferous dancing." She also continually blamed the theatre for attracting the thief who had stabbed her husband fifteen years earlier.

"You need to get into an honest trade," she told Wat, who was at home after the play at the Rose, hoping that Anne would appear. "You'll never get anywhere with those scurvy players."

"Mr. Alleyn has a fine house, and is really a gentleman," Wat said.

"Henslowe has to bail one of those players out of debtor's prison every week. And they're always brawling at the taverns."

"You like John Pig." Wat had brought the young actor home with him one day.

"My John would still be alive if decent people were around the playhouses, instead of cutpurses and vagabonds. And what about old Timothy Rudd, with his head split open?"

"You and the Captain liked the play last week well enough."

Mrs. Simpkin had some reason for her concern. Although most of the actors were serious about their work and honest citizens, neither players nor playwrights earned much money. Henslowe was constantly making advances to writers or lending small sums to actors in some kind of trouble. It was also true that some of the great number of rogues and vagabonds that infested London did frequent the playhouses, especially nips, who carried knives and cut off purses, and foists, who considered themselves more skillful artists and lifted purses from pockets. Both nips and foists usually worked with a stall, whose business was to jostle and perplex a victim while his purse was being removed.

Before Mrs. Simpkin could press her argument further, she saw Anne outside the door and hurried to let her in. Anne greeted Wat shyly, and Wat stood quietly and admiringly as she completed her errand to the widow.

"I suppose you'll let this one walk home with you," Mrs. Simpkin said. "But you'd better try to keep him away from that playhouse."

Anne and Wat both nodded respectfully and set off for the Mitre.

By 1597 tavern life had become very popular in London; alehouses were sometimes rowdy but also were centers for discussion, especially gathering places for poets and players. The Boar's Head in Eastcheap was known as a tavern at least as early as 1537. The Dagger in Holburn was not close to the Bankside theatres and attracted few players; it was known for its strong Dagger ale and had a reputation as a gambling house often frequented by disreputable characters. The Mitre and the Mermaid, both in Cheapside, were rivals, both catering for poets and players and patrons of the theatres.

Wat didn't often eat at the Mitre, partly because meals were paid for with his rent at Mrs. Simpkin's and partly because Anne didn't seem to want him joining the fairly rowdy crowds, especially after plays. The players from the Rose weren't regulars at the Mitre; and on the few occasions when Wat had tried to prove his adulthood by joining them, they had gone for ale or sack at the Mermaid or one of the other taverns. But as Wat entered the Mitre with Anne, he saw at once a group of his fellows who had obviously been keeping the tapster busy for some time. Towne was there and Ed Juby and John Singer and Thomas Hearne, who had just been hired. Towne called to Wat, and Anne hurried off to the apartment above the tavern. There were tankards of ale on the table and three or four pipes of tobacco; the players made a place for Wat. Wat was flattered, but the center of attention was young John Pig, who had just finished a song and was being loudly applauded. Wat observed fairly quickly that there was a purpose behind their flattery of Pig and perhaps also their quick welcome to him. Pig, as a favorite of Joan Alleyn, was often present when the Alleyns were talking about theater. Towne especially was trying to pump Pig.

"Have another, Johnny" he said as Wat joined the group, "and bring one for Wat here."

Wat accepted the bumper and tried to drink as if he were a regular at the Mitre. Being accepted as part of the company was a little heady for both boys. Towne continued.

"I'll wager Johnny here could tell us some things about what goes on in high places. Am I right, Johnny?"

Pig smiled knowingly. "I know a thing or two."

John Singer jumped in. "Have you heard anything about that new play of the Chamberlain's, *Richard*?

"There's talk." Pig was enjoying the attention.

"What about?"

"They say the Queen doesn't like it. Burbage and the others may be in trouble."

"I heard a ballad singer the other day hawking something he called "The Deposing and Murder of King Richard II," Singer added. "There's talk around town."

"Did the Council officer ask you about that?" Towne turned to Wat. "Or about the Earl of Essex?"

"He asked if I'd heard talk about Essex," Wat said, "but I hadn't."

"What do you hear, Johnny?"

"Some people think the Council is looking for somebody in one of the companies, somebody who may be a traitor. They think old Timothy knew something?"

"Do they mention names? Anybody mention me?" Towne laughed.

Johnny laughed and shook his head.

"You've not the courage to be a traitor, Tom," Juby said. "You've too much allegiance to sack and ale."

Hearne had been drinking quietly, but he broke in. "Who was this man Rudd, who was killed before I came in from the country?"

"He was just a handyman around the Rose," Singer said. "Young Wat here found his body."

"Why was he killed?"

"Nobody knows that," said Singer. "He probably knew something dangerous."

"What did he do before he came to the theatre?" Hearne asked.

"Nobody knows that either," Singer said.

"I have to be up early," Hearne said, and he emptied his tankard and left.

Juby waved his empty tankard. "More ale here! How about another song, Johnny, and some more ale?"

Pig obliged with a popular ballad with a bad pun for its title, "The Ex-Ale-tation of Ale," with the group joining in on the chorus line, "Much virtue there is in a pot of good ale." The verses seemed endless; the crowd tired before John did.

"That's enough, Young Johnny," Towne said. "But thank you, and here's to your health."

The party concentrated on drinking, and Towne apparently decided he had all the information Pig could supply.

"Why did Hearne leave so early?" Juby asked. "Do you know where he's living?"

"I don't know anything about him," said Towne, "but he seems to know his business. Do you know where he played in the country?"

"I never saw him in the country," Juby said. "But Ed Tobye may have known him."

Singer changed the subject. "Have you seen the new doxies hanging around the Mermaid?"

Wat and Johnny were fascinated but slightly embarrassed by the new discussion. They listened for a while, then left relishing the raucous farewells. Both of them were a little tipsy. Pig grinned as they walked out of the tavern.

"I didn't tell them," he said, "that Mr. Alleyn thinks somebody in the company, maybe Slater, is stealing play copies and selling them to a bookseller who's printing pirated editions."

Chapter Five

❦

𝔄 𝔖𝔥𝔬𝔱 𝔦𝔫 𝔱𝔥𝔢 𝔏𝔞𝔰𝔱 𝔄𝔠𝔱

WAT ARRIVED at the Rose early as usual on July 18. There was no performance scheduled, but Alleyn had called the company for a rehearsal of *The Spanish Tragedy*, Thomas Kyd's 1585 tragedy which the Admiral's Men had already revived half a dozen times during the year. In the theatre it had come to be called *Jeronimo*, for the name of its hero. Wat had no role in the old play, but he thought he might be useful with props or costumes during the rehearsal.

Most of the company had appeared in an hour.

"How long can we keep doing this ancient piece of fustian?" asked Singer, looking at the prompter's plot attached to a post in the tiring house.

"The groundlings still love it," said Juby. "I heard a ballad monger just the other day singing the doggerel made from the play, set to the tune of Queen Dido. Whoever made that ballad must have seen Mr. Alleyn."

"And why is that?" Alleyn asked. Juby hadn't noticed that he had come in.

"A couple of lines from the ballad go like this," said Juby.
"Then vexed more I stamp'd and frown'd
And with my poignard ript the ground.
That's what you do."

"That may be," said Alleyn, "but we need to get the rehearsal started."

He started checking the cast. "Where's Balthazar? Ed Tobye," he called. "You're on early in the first act."

Henslowe came in, making an unusual early appearance. The

group became quiet. "I want to let you know that Martin Slater and Ed Tobye have left the company," he said. He turned and left without further comment. The announcement apparently was news to Alleyn as well as the others.

"I'm not surprised about Slater," said Towne. "He has an errant eye. I thought he'd be leaving, even though he had a good part as Theodore in *Frederick and Basilea*. We haven't done the play in a month, and it wasn't very successful. Slater should have stayed in the country."

"But what about Tobye?" asked Ed Juby. "He's been playing Balthazar in *Jeronimo*.

"He's been pretty quiet lately," Towne said, "And he was talking a long time with the two officers from the Queen's Council when they were here to question Wat. Did you see them with Tobye, Wat?"

"No," said Wat. He wondered whether Tobye's early morning look at the site of old Tim's murder meant anything

"Well, they were probably trying not to be seen. Tobye looked to me like he was afraid of something."

"We don't really know much about Tobye," said Singer. "Where did he act before he came to us? He wasn't with any of the troupes in the country."

"We'll have to shift some assignments," Alleyn said. "Wat, do you think you could do something with Balthazar by tomorrow?"

Wat jumped. This was a much larger part than he had ever tried, and learning it perfectly by the next day was impossible. "I'd like to try," Wat said.

"Here's the script for Balthazar's part. We can run through it during the rehearsal. Use the script, and the prompter will help you with business."

Then he turned to the rest of the cast. "We'll all need to review our lines, and put in some additions that Mr. Henslowe commissioned. Most of the new lines are for Jeronimo, and I'm working on them, but there are some for Isabella." He turned to Will Barne. "Here is the part for your additions."

Wat was excited and a little frightened; he went off to a corner of the stage to take a look at the lines. He had seen the earlier performances of the play and remembered the role of Balthazar. John Pig followed him. "Congratulations," he said. "You'll have it down by tomorrow's performance." Then he pulled Wat behind one of the stage posts and whispered, "I bet Mr. Alleyn was right about Slater stealing play books." And Pig walked off. He had a major role in *Jeronimo* as the heroine, Bel-imperia.

The rehearsal started in about half an hour with the chorus, Revenge and the Ghost of Andrea, speaking from the upper stage. Andrea had been murdered by Balthazar, and his ghost wants revenge. Juby and Towne were double cast, Juby doing Andrea's Ghost and the Viceroy of Portugal and Towne playing Revenge and the Portuguese Ambassador. Their lines rang out smoothly, with no pauses or slips, partly because they could use hidden scripts sheltered by the railing of the upper stage. Juby as the Ghost did a rousing recitation of his experience in the underworld, including accounts of tortures he observed on his way to Pluto's court, usurers "choked with melting gold," wantons "embraced with ugly snakes."

Wat appeared in the first act, brought in as a captive by Horatio, played by James Dunstone, and Lorenzo, the brother of Bel-Imperia and villain of the piece. There was clearly no part in the play for a comic actor, but Singer took the role of the villain as the next best assignment for him and was an ominous and evil Lorenzo.

The play moved easily through the first act, with Horatio and Bel-imperia lamenting the death of Andrea and Wat getting his first chance at a love scene as Balthazar woos Bel-imperia with elaborate double talk. In an aside he declares that he is "slain by beauty's tyranny," although Bel-imperia is devoted to Horatio. Revenge closes Act I, promising that he'll turn love to hate and peace to war.

Wat had long speeches as Balthazar and Lorenzo open Act II by discovering that Bel-imperia loves Horatio and deciding that

Balthazar can prosper in his suit only if Horatio is out of the way. With Lorenzo in charge they find Horatio and Bel-imperia telling each other of their love. They stab Horatio and hang him in the arbor, where Jeronimo, Horatio's father, finds him. Jeronimo and his wife Isabella, lament their son's death. Alleyn interrupted the rehearsal at this stage to introduce new lines, with Jeronimo approaching madness in the extravagance of his grief. Alleyn and Will Barne as Isabella read the lines without restraint.

"Can the audience take any more of this kind of stuff?" John Singer whispered.

"They'll love it," said Juby.

The Ghost is disappointed that Balthazar is still alive, but Revenge promises to take care of Balthazar.

Wat had a short rest at the start of Act III, as Jeronimo continues his lament; but then Balthazar and Lorenzo guess that Jeronimo may know of their guilt. They provide a pistol for the servant Pedringano, one of their two confederates in the murder, and bribe him to shoot Serberine, the other possible witness. Pedringano is caught and threatens to reveal their guilt if he is not saved from hanging, but he is hanged. Jeronimo continues to express his grief and vow revenge, now fully aware that Balthazar and Lorenzo are guilty. Even in rehearsal Alleyn boomed the lines, and Wat realized why Alleyn was a favorite of the groundlings.

The rehearsal went on, getting rougher and rougher, not only because Wat was new in one of the big roles but because everyone was rusty on lines they had not used for a month. The additions added to the confusion, a whole new scene in Act IV.

"This has nothing to do with the play," said Towne as a new character, a painter, was introduced. "There's no reason for this except to milk a little more sentimentality out of Horatio's death."

"It'll play well," said Thomas Downton, who had taken on an additional role as the painter, who has also lost a son and can join Jeronimo in grieving.

"We'll leave it in," said Alleyn, "even though it may be more than enough. It establishes Jeronimo's madness."

They got through the rest of the act, with everybody tired and less than enthusiastic about the old play—except for Wat who remained excited about his first big role. The Ghost and Revenge closed the act.

The performance the next day would go on without any intermissions, but Alleyn called for a break after the fourth act. "Let's take half an hour," he said, "and look over your lines for the last act. Maybe we can keep it from dragging the way the first four have. I know you don't know the lines, Wat, but see if you can pick up the cues a little faster. And Singer, remember that Lorenzo is not a comic character."

The last act did pick up, with Jeronimo enlisting his enemies as actors in a play within the play, destined to implement his revenge and get most of the characters killed. Isabella goes mad in scene ii before Jeronimo's play starts and stabs herself in the arbor where Horatio died. The play within the play proceeds quickly as a marathon of violent deaths, with characters unaware that the stabbing is real, not play-acting. Jeronimo stabs Lorenzo. Then Balthazar turns to declare his love for Bel-imperia. Wat didn't remember much of this encounter from performances he had seen, but he decided to kneel before Bel-imperia to plead his love and wait for her to stab him and then herself. Just as he knelt, there was a loud bang from the inner stage, and Wat heard a bullet whistle over his head into a pillar. A door slammed; there were shouts and sounds of running feet through the tiring house. Wat stood up and shook his head.

The rehearsal was over. The company was in complete confusion. It was established that nobody had been hurt, but people were scurrying through the tiring house looking for any strangers. People were shouting for the watch. Alleyn tried to restore a little order.

"We'll not try to finish the rehearsal," he said. "But will everybody in Act V come in early to run through the new scene. Let's all go home and let the watch deal with this." He saw Constable Slocum making another entrance into the Rose.

"Well, at least," commented Towne, "we won't have to suffer that final scene until tomorrow, with Alleyn spitting out a piece of bloody pig's liver, and all the groundlings thinking it's his tongue."

"You just don't appreciate sophisticated theatre," said Singer. "I'd be interested to see that pistol that Pedringano used in the third act."

"What about a pistol?" said Constable Slocum, who had come in just in time to hear the remark.

"Props," Alleyn called. Tom Downton's boy, who had been handling properties hurried in. "Where's the Act III pistol?"

"I put it back in the property room as soon as the scene was over, but it's gone."

"Find it." said Alleyn. Slocum nodded agreement.

"Who was in front of that post when the shot was fired?" Slocum asked; and then as Wat stepped forward, "I've seen you before."

"Yes sir," Wat said.

"Why would somebody be shooting at you, and not a very good marksman?"

"I don't know."

Slocum took a look at the post behind Wat. "There's a bullet here, all right." He pulled a knife from his pocket and pried the ball loose. "Could this have come from that pistol?"

Downton's boy came back. "It's gone," he said. "I can't find it anywhere. But it never had any real bullets in it."

"Maybe somebody put a real bullet in it," Slocum said. "Did any of you see who fired the shot?"

There was total silence. Even Towne and Singer resisted any temptation to comment.

"Well, I guess nobody was hurt, and you're pretty lucky." He turned to Wat. "But there's something funny going on in this theatre, and the Queen's Council is going to be interested."

Slocum left.

"If anybody finds that gun, I want to know about it at once," said Alleyn. "Whoever fired the shot must have got away through the tiring house; but if anybody saw anything unusual, I want

him to come to me. And remember, there are changes in the final
scene, and I want the King and Castile and the Viceroy to come in
early and run over the new lines with me."

He called Wat aside. "You need to be careful, Wat. Somebody
may think still that you know something about old Timothy's
murder. Or somebody may not have known that you had taken
Tobye's place. You're doing fine in the part. Go home and work on
your lines."

Wat went to his room to study, but he had trouble concentrat-
ing on himself as Balthazar rather than as a target for someone who
couldn't shoot straight.

Chapter Six

❦

The Return of Tobye

THE NEW LINES did not make significant changes in the final scene, mostly adding to the gory climax in which Alleyn as Jeronimo is threatened with torture if he refuses to reveal information about the deaths of Balthazar and Bel-imperia. Jeronimo bites out his tongue and spits it on the stage so that he cannot talk—the scene Towne had ridiculed, with a piece of liver masquerading as Jeronimo's tongue. The King then orders him to write the truth. Jeronimo asks for a knife to mend his pen but uses the knife to stab the Duke and himself. Alleyn had carried off this climax dozens of times and could manage the new lines without a full rehearsal. He and the last-act principals had the new lines after an hour's work and were ready for Revenge to close the play:

This hand shall hale them down to deepest hell,
Where none but furies, bugs, and tortures dwell.

Alleyn left, but most of the others in the cast had come in early, eager to talk about yesterday's shooting. They all seemed to talk at once, some of them clustering around Wat and Johnny Pig and others speculating about why Wat had been the target. Their talk was interrupted as they heard shouts from the yard, then sounds of running. The door from the stage burst open and Will Kempe rushed in, out of breath.

Alleyn came back on to the stage. "What are you doing here, Will Kempe," he asked. "Don't they have anything for you to do over at the Curtain?"

Kempe wiped his brow on his sleeve. "Haven't you heard the news? We may all be in for it. The Council's closed the Swan, and there's talk that all the theatres will be closed."

The Swan, like the Bear Garden and the Rose, had been built on the Bankside south of the Thames, on property owned by the Crown. Therefore, like the other theatres, it was free from the jurisdiction of the Lord Mayor and the aldermen of London, but subject to the Queen's Council. The City officials had recently renewed their criticisms of the theatres after some unruly apprentices confessed that plays had served as the "randevous" of their "mutinus attemptes."

Kempe's audience was suddenly attentive, although they knew Kempe well enough to wonder whether this was one of his bad jokes. "Why the Swan?" asked John Singer. "You're the ones with the Richard play the Queen objects to."

"It's a new play by Tom Nashe, just opened today. It's called *The Isle of Dogs*, and the Council seems able to figure out too well who some of the dogs are supposed to be. Some think the play mocks the Polish ambassador, who had a bout with the Queen last week. Some think one of the canine characters represents Cecil and think some of the Essex faction are behind it."

"That sounds bad," said Towne. "Is Nashe in trouble?"

"Nobody knows. He seems to have disappeared. But Ben Jonson, who helped with the writing, is in the Marshalsea, along with Gabriel Spencer and Robert Shaw from Pembroke's Men."

"Did Edmund Tilney approve the play for performance?" said Henslowe, who had come in when he heard the excitement. "He should know better than to pass a play with sedition in it." Edmund Tilney, Master of the Revels, had been in office many years and was responsible for licensing plays.

"He must have allowed it," Alleyn said.

"There'll be a lot of out-of-work actors looking for jobs," Henslowe said.

"I hope we're not among them," said Singer.

Kempe enjoyed being the center of attention, but he was obviously a little concerned about the reference to the Richard play. He turned to Singer. "What have you heard about the Richard play?"

"What everybody hears. That the Queen doesn't like a play about a successful usurper. And I hear too that Cecil thinks you have some people working for Essex."

Towne added a question. "Didn't the Council officer question you about old Timothy Rudd? What were you doing here that morning?"

Kempe answered only with a little dance step, commenting as he left, "I wish us all luck."

"We'd best go on our ways," said Alleyn. "But let's all come in early in the morning. Mr. Henslowe and I'll try to find out tonight what's going on. I think we'll be all right and can count on a performance tomorrow."

Alleyn was less confident than he sounded. He knew that Henslowe had been able to keep the Rose open in spite of the City's objections because the Queen and her Council were supporters of the plays and turned a blind eye to the alleged abuses pointed out by Puritans and other critics. But *The Isle of Dogs* looked like interference in politics and criticism of the government, with possibilities of causing civil commotion. The Council could not overlook that.

Alleyn would have been still more worried had he known details of a letter from the Privy Council addressed to the Justices of Middlesex and Surrey ordering that playhouses "shall be plucked down." Another letter from the Council was addressed to the person who had first called the attention of the Council to that "seditious play," the *Isle of Dogs*, the famous heretic-hunter Richard Topcliffe. Topcliffe was given a commission to ascertain how far the "lewd" play had been spread abroad and also to examine players who might be involved in "lewd and mutinous behavior."

Wat went off to the Mitre, hoping to tell Anne about his new part and his escape from the bullet. She wasn't there, but he found her just returning from Mrs. Simpkin's. They walked along the Thames, and Wat reported on the events at the theatre, not minimizing the danger he had been in. Anne was satisfactorily sympathetic.

"You might have been killed," she said, and took his hand.

Wat saw his advantage and added details of the shooting, including his luck in kneeling just as the shot was fired.

"Mr. Alleyn thought somebody might not have known I was taking Tobye's place and meant the bullet for him."

"I heard something about that," Anne said. "When I was with Joan Alleyn earlier today, she said Mr. Alleyn was worried about the actors who had left the company. He's pretty sure one of them was selling play scripts to a printer. And the other may be some kind of spy."

"Johnny Pig heard something like that too."

"You must be careful, Wat. I don't want anything to happen to you."

Wat was feeling very good as he went on home to work on the Balthazar part, and even managed to feel a little like a hero as he told Mrs. Simpkin and the Captain about his escape.

"You should start carrying a sword," said the Captain. "A man needs to be ready with all the whoreson rogues around. I can show you how to sink a blade in any cowardly cur using an axe."

"He'll do no such thing," said the widow. "You and your big talk. But you be careful, Wat."

Wat went off to his room to study lines and get to bed early. He was up at dawn, as always eager to get to the theatre early. He thought some of the cast would be in to go over the final scene again. He found the main entrance to the Rose standing open, so he went in walking through the pit, rather than going around to the door into the tiring house. The stage was still in half darkness, and props for *Jeronimo*, including the gallows in the garden, had an eerie look. Wat thought for a minute that the Captain might be right about his learning to use a sword. He walked up on the main stage, still feeling something ominous in the total silence. Then suddenly he heard a muffled scream and a dull thud, apparently from the upper stage. For a moment he was unable to move. He was about to call out, but then it seemed to him wiser not to let anybody know he was there. He moved quietly toward the balcony stairs, frightened but curious about what was going on. As he started up the stairs, he heard a scraping noise, as if someone was dragging a heavy object across the floor of the upper stage. And then as he reached the top of the stairs he saw a dim figure, apparently wearing some kind of mask, pulling a man or a man's body back into the shadows.

Wat was not feeling heroic, but almost automatically he moved up to the stage, shouting for help as he ran. The masked figure dropped his burden and rushed for the stairs, hitting Wat as he passed with a blow to the head hard enough to knock him down and momentarily stun him. By the time Wat had recovered enough to follow he could see only a dim figure running through the pit and then disappearing through the gate.

Wat called again for help, and then looked at what had caused the scraping sound. A man with a broken head was lying in a pool of blood. A track of blood marked where the body had been dragged, apparently in an attempt to pull it behind a curtain. He turned the head so that he could see the face and recognized Ed Tobye, who along with Martin Slater, had left the company the day before. It was Tobye's part in *Jeronimo* that Wat had taken over; the shot that had interrupted the rehearsal might have been meant for Tobye.

Wat's continuing shouts for help got no response from the tiring house; but after a few minutes his calls outside the gate got a response from a few loitering apprentices and finally brought Constable Philip Slocum and a small crowd into the theatre.

"He looks dead," said Slocum.

Slocum examined the body and then picked up the bloody axe lying near it.

"Is this yours?" he asked Wat.

"I never saw it," said Wat. "Maybe it came from inside where workmen left it."

Slocum walked around some more. "You make a habit of finding bodies?"

Wat saw no reason to answer.

"It looks like he was just killed. Let's have a look at your hands."

Wat looked at his hands. He had got blood on them when he turned Tobye's head. Slocum smiled with satisfaction.

"That seems to be pretty good evidence. Why did you kill him? Can anybody identify the body?"

The crowd on the stage had grown, and Wat noticed Towne and Juby and other members of the company who had come in for the rehearsal.

"I think his name is Ed Tobye," Wat said. "He left the company yesterday. But I had nothing to do with killing him. I heard a noise on the upper stage when I came in. Nobody answered when I called, so I went up the stairs to see who was there. Someone with a mask was trying to drag the body behind a curtain. He knocked me down, and when I got up, I heard someone running. I ran down trying to catch him, but he got through the gate and disappeared."

"Who was it?" Slocum asked.

"I couldn't see. The light was bad and he wore a mask."

"That's an interesting story, but you're the one with the bloody hands."

"I got blood on them when I turned his head to see who it was."

"We'll let Carlin, the Queen's Council man, think about that. You are to stay around here till he comes. Why did Tobye leave the company?"

Towne stepped in. "He and another actor, Martin Slater, were going to join a company in the country," he said.

"Is this Slater here?" Slocum asked.

"He probably left London," Juby said.

"The Privy Council and Lord Burghley will want to know about this," Slocum said.

And he was right. Slocum, with an attempt at exerting authority, announced that nobody in the company was to leave London and that everybody was a suspect in the murder. And before noon William Carlin, the agent for the Council, close to Robert Cecil, arrived at the theatre and began questioning everybody in the company. Wat was questioned much as he had been when old Timothy had been killed—about why he was in the theatre so early, how well he knew Tobye, how well he knew Martin Slater and Will Kempe and Thomas Towne, and finally what he heard about the Earl of Essex. Carlin had Wat go over his account of hearing noises on the upper stage and seeing someone run out of the theatre. Apparently Carlin accepted his story.

Carlin spent a long time with Henslowe and Alleyn trying to decide whether the Admiral's Men had anything to do with *The Isle of Dogs* at the Swan. Alleyn announced that the afternoon performance of *Jeronimo* was postponed, but that the theatres would not all be closed, as Kempe had predicted. Benjamin Jonson and Gabriel Spencer remained in jail, but the Council seemed to have forgotten its earlier harsh orders, at least for the Admiral's Men. Wat was glad to have extra time to work on his new part, and he was glad that the Rose would open in a day or two.

He worked on his lines that night until he fell asleep, and then continued in the morning, helped some of the time by Anne. The next day he was at the theatre by noon, ready for his first big role. And the postponed performance of *Jeronimo*, with revisions and with Wat in the role of Balthazar, was a success. Wat managed to get through the play without too much help from the prompter.

"Nobody pays much heed to the lines anyway, when they're watching this piece," said John Pig as they walked toward the Mitre tavern after the play. "The stinkards are just waiting to see all that pig's blood and the piece of liver Alleyn spits out at the end."

"Be glad it wasn't John Pig's blood," said Wat.

It had been a noisy audience. A big gang of apprentices had managed to get out for the afternoon to keep both the Rose and the ale houses alert and busy. A few pieces of orange peel had been thrown on the stage, and the actors had plenty of shouted encouragement whenever there was a chance of some kind of violent action. Singer, playing an ominously evil Lorenzo, got almost as much attention as Alleyn and was pleased about it. He was standing outside the Mitre when Wat and Johnny approached it.

"A fine job, Wat," he said. "We villains are the ones they come to see. I think I'm going to give up being a comic."

"They cheered when Johnny stabbed me, but more when Jeronimo finished you," Wat said.

"When is another performance scheduled?" Pig asked.

"Next week, I think," said Singer. The humors play is on tomorrow. How about going in for a pint to celebrate. I'll buy."

They found Ed Juby and Tom Towne already drinking.

"Come join us," called Towne. "But try not to find any bodies under the table, Wat."

"I don't want to be shot at either," said Juby.

"Nor do I," said Wat.

"What does Alleyn think about it, Johnny?" Towne asked, still hoping Pig had inside information on what Alleyn or Henslowe had found out. "Have they found the gun?"

"I don't think so," said Pig. "I think Slocum and Mr. Carlin from the Council looked all through the theatre."

"It was probably somebody from outside who didn't know Wat had taken over for Tobye," said Towne. "Obviously somebody was after Tobye. Maybe somebody from the Chamberlain's Men. Will Kempe has been showing up here a lot."

"What about Slater?" asked Singer. "I hear he's been stealing play scripts for the printers. Maybe Tobye knew what he was doing, and Slater wanted to keep him quiet. He wouldn't have known that Tobye had left the company too."

"Or what about Tom Hearne?" asked Juby. "He just signed on and he's not in *Jeronimo*. He might not have known about the cast change."

"I haven't seen him for two days," Towne said.

Hearne had contracted just a few weeks earlier to play for the Admiral's Men for two years. But nobody knew him very well.

"Where was he playing before he turned up here?" Juby went on. "Somebody said he spent some time in the country, but none of us knew him. Somebody else thought he was with a troupe on the continent."

"But why would he have wanted to kill Tobye?" Singer asked. "I suppose he could have known him in the past, but I never saw them together. Slater might have had a reason."

"But what was Tobye doing back at the Rose? And how would Hearne or Slater or anybody else know he'd be there?"

Juby shook his head and noticed that his tankard was empty.

"Maybe that shot was meant for you after all, Wat." Towne was only half serious. "Carlin, the Council investigator, seems to think you know something. Did he ask you about Essex again."

"He did," said Wat. "I don't know anything, but I'm being careful."

"We all need to be careful," Singer said. "Jonson is still in the Marshalsea, and Pembroke's Men are no longer playing. Gabriel Spencer and Robert Shaw, I hear, are looking to join us."

"Something strange does seem to be going on." said Juby. "I keep remembering that only four years ago Tom Kyd was tortured when he was accused of atheism. I think Carlin had something to do with that. And Kit Marlowe, drinking in the Golden Hind at Deptford, was stabbed in the head and died swearing. It's not always healthy being a player."

Chapter Seven

A Queen's Council Agent

WILL CARLIN would have agreed. He had been working for half a dozen years as a special agent for Lord Burghley and more lately for his son, Robert Cecil, and most of his assignments had involved the acting companies or others connected with the theatres. He had had his first big assignments in 1593 when he investigated the complaints against playwright Thomas Kyd, whose *Spanish Tragedy*, now being revived as *Jeronimo*, was a current favorite with audiences at the Rose. Even after torture nothing was ever proved against Kyd, and the atheism charges were not pursued. But Carlin's efforts did cause embarrassment to some of Kyd's friends, including Ralegh and others in the court.

The other 1593 assignment had got more complicated. He was called in to investigate the death of Christopher Marlowe, who was stabbed in the head at Deptford, where Francis Drake's old ship, the *Golden Hind*, had been tied up and made into a tavern. There were witnesses, and Carlin hounded them until he finally could name one Ingram Frizer as the killer. And then he discovered that Frizer was an employee of Sir Thomas Walsingham, who had important friends at court. He had to drop the investigation, and Frizer was acquitted on grounds of self defense.

Carlin was just over thirty years old, tall and thin, a Londoner by birth, who knew his way around the Bankside. He was unmarried, and his acquaintance in the stews around the theatres often served him well in his work as well as his pleasure. He lived alone and had no close friends, but he was trusted by officers of the Queen and was increasingly prosperous.

His interests in the theatres in 1597 had nothing to do with the constant complaints from Puritans about the immorality of the stage, the harlots in the audience, and the evils of having men dressed in women's clothes. The Council managed to pretend to take these complaints seriously but to ignore them. And he was not concerned about pirated editions of plays; the companies could take care of such matters. He was not even concerned about the murders at the Rose except as results of what he considered more important crimes. The death of old Timothy Rudd needed investigation only because of possible reasons for his murder. Tobye's murder was more puzzling. Carlin did not think it had anything to do with Martin Slater or stolen play manuscripts. He did think it had some connection with the murder of old Timothy and perhaps with his main interests in the activities of London actors.

Carlin was sure that he was going to uncover something seditious in one of the companies, some kind of treason even more important than the Kyd and Marlowe affairs. If he could really find a plot against the Queen, he'd have some standing in the court. He was fairly sure that Tobye had been involved somehow. But he still wasn't sure what he'd found out with the *Isle of Dogs* affair. Certainly there had been treasonous material in the play, and Gabriel Spencer and Ben Jonson had been apprehended, but Thomas Nashe, supposedly the main author, had disappeared, and nobody seemed much concerned to try to find him or to push the charges against the two in jail. Carlin didn't think any of these were Catholics, and he was looking for something big like the Babington plot.

He was watching Will Kempe and Thomas Pope of the Chamberlain's company, although he had no real reason for suspecting them. Kempe, for no good reason, had managed to be present soon after both murders. He found Thomas Towne of the Admiral's Men more curious about the murders than he had reason to be. He found it suspicious that nobody knew anything about what Tobye and Slater and Thomas Hearne had been doing before they came to the Rose. And he couldn't quite be sure whether Wat was as naive as he seemed. He wondered about Wat's

connection with old Captain Daglish, who had been involved in
an Irish campaign years ago and might still have some political
interests.

Carlin wasn't even sure that the shot during the last act of the
Jeronimo rehearsal had been intended for Tobye rather than Wat.
The murderer couldn't be sure that Wat hadn't seen somebody
when he discovered old Timothy Rudd with his head smashed. Or
Wat might have heard something around the theatre that somebody considered dangerous. He was friendly with young Pig, who
had easy access to the Alleyns. He was obviously interested in Anne
Page, a friend of Joan Alleyn, Henslowe's daughter. And he was
probably naive enough about London politics to hear things without knowing what they meant. Carlin's quiet persistence was one
of the qualities that made him the Council's chief investigator. He
decided to talk to Wat again.

This time he called at the widow Simpkin's. Wat hadn't returned
from the theatre, but Mrs. Simpkin and the Captain were there,
and Carlin asked if he could wait.

Daglish was at work on his afternoon ale and asked Carlin to
join him.

"How long have you known young Wat?" Carlin asked.

"Since he first came to London," said the Captain. "I'faith, he's a
fine young man, good enough for the navy."

"What do you think?" Carlin turned to Mrs. Simpkin.

"Aye, a fine lad. It's too bad he can't do better for himself than
be mixed up with those players. That's how my husband went,
many years ago."

"What happened?" Carlin asked.

"He was a fine man, John Simpkin, and a good member of the
watch. But he got called to the Curtain one afternoon just because
of a purse snatcher, and two or three rogues set upon him and
stabbed him to death. Rogues and vagabonds, cutpurses and foists,
that's what they are."

"Do any of the players come here with Wat?"

"Only a lad called Johnny Pig. And he seems a fine boy like Wat."

But you never can tell with that lot."

Wat came in at this point. He seemed surprised and a little flustered to see Carlin there, but he greeted him politely and asked if he could help. Carlin went over the same questions he had asked before, trying especially to get Wat to remember more details about the man he had seen running out of the theatre. Then he tried some new topics.

"Do you think that shot at rehearsal was meant for Tobye or for you?"

"I can't think of any reason anyone would shoot at me."

"Are you still sure you didn't see anyone or anything that morning when you found old Timothy Rudd? Somebody may think you could have incriminating information."

"I didn't see anyone or anything. I called out several times, but nobody seemed to be around."

"What about Tobye's killer? You were close enough to him to get knocked down. What did he look like?"

"He had a mask on, and I didn't get a good look at him. I've tried to think whether he looked like anyone I know."

"Couldn't you recognize the way he ran or his size?"

"I couldn't recognize anything."

Carlin shifted his approach. "How well do you know Will Kempe from the Chamberlain's Men?"

"As I told you, I never talked to him. I just saw him once on the stage at the Curtain."

"That's the worst of all of those places," Mrs. Simpkin observed.

"Did you ever talk to Kempe's friend, Thomas Pope?"

"No," said Wat.

"How well do you know Martin Slater?"

"I saw him with the other actors. We were all in a group at the Mitre one time. But I never talked to him alone."

"Did you know he was suspected of stealing plays?"

"Johnny Pig told me."

Carlin shifted again. "What do you hear about the Earl of Essex?"

"I hear he's leading an expedition against the Spanish."

"You didn't tell me that when I asked you before. Who told you that?"

"I can't remember anyone. It was just talked about in the theatre. Maybe it was Towne or Juby. I didn't pay much attention."

Carlin wasn't sure whether it was unusual for the actors to know about the Essex expedition, but he decided Wat couldn't know anything dangerous about it. He thanked Mrs. Simpkin for the ale.

"And you be careful, Wat," he said as he left.

Carlin decided that he had to know more about Ed Tobye before he could make any progress. He was pretty sure that Tobye had had some kind of political connection, but he had not seen him working with any of the other Council agents. He could have been working with Essex's followers, but that didn't seem likely. Carlin decided to start with Edward Alleyn and Henslowe.

Henslowe was not much help. He had hired Tobye earlier in the year on a recommendation from Martin Slater, who had known him when they were both acting in the country. Unlike most of the actors, he had never asked for any loans or advances on salary. When Carlin pressed this point, Henslowe said that Tobye seemed to have no problems about money and might have had some other source of income. Henslowe confirmed that printers were publishing plays without authorization, but he could not be sure that Slater or Tobye or anybody else had been stealing manuscripts. Someone might have been taking manuscripts to printers and returning them before they were missed. Or printers might have got copies from shorthand transcripts taken during performances, perhaps with help from some player's part script. Some of the pirated copies were garbled enough to suggest a shorthand source for the text.

"Why did Tobye and Slater decide to leave the company?" Carlin asked. "Wasn't it rather sudden?"

"Tobye said he had a chance at a better job. He wouldn't say anything about it, but I got an impression he would be working for somebody of influence. Slater said he was going with a troupe into the country, which is maybe where he belongs. He's not a very good actor."

Carlin found Alleyn at the theatre and talked to him in Henslowe's office.

"Tobye was obviously an experienced actor," Alleyn said. "But I don't know much about his background. He had acted in the country. He was quiet, caused no trouble. Didn't seem to have close friends, except maybe Slater, but he was pleasant enough."

"Could he have been some kind of spy?" Carlin asked.

"I suppose he could have been, but I saw no evidence of it."

"Do you think that shot during the rehearsal the other day was intended for him rather than young Wat?"

"I don't know. Somebody might still think Wat knows something about the murders. I've told him to be careful."

"Would everybody in the company have known that Wat had taken Tobye's part in the play?"

"I think everybody in our company knew. Possibly Tom Hearne didn't know. He had just joined us and had not been in for a day or two."

"Could Wat Gayton be connected with the Essex faction? There've been some ambitious young gallants even out of Tunbridge."

"No, that's ridiculous," Alleyn said. "Wat's a stage-struck lad who hardly knows that Essex exists."

Carlin shifted the subject again. "Do you know Ben Jonson, the one who's still in the Marshalsea?"

"Yes, I know him. But not well. Henslowe's paid him for some writing, I think."

"What did you think of that *Isle of Dogs* play?"

"I didn't see it. I just know that some of your people didn't approve of it."

"Could Tobye have learned something about some of Essex's followers, enough to get his head smashed? Was he friendly with any of the players at the Curtain?"

"I suppose he could have. And many of the players in London

know each other. There's a lot of moving about from one company to another."

"Could somebody from the Chamberlain's company have slipped in during the rehearsal the other day and fired that shot at young Gayton? Did you see any of them around?"

"Anyone could have slipped in. But I didn't see any of the Chamberlain's players."

"What about Will Kempe? Wasn't he here that day?"

"He came in after the shooting to tell us about *The Isle of Dogs*. I suppose he could have been here earlier, but I didn't see him."

"Why did Tobye and Slater decide to leave the company? Did they talk to you about it?"

"No. I was surprised when Mr. Henslowe announced that they were going. Especially Tobye. He had a good part in *Jeronimo,* and was usually reliable. Nobody seems to know what he planned."

"How about Slater?"

"That's a different story. I'm quite sure that Slater has been involved somehow with a stationer named John Danter, who has been putting out play quartos not authorized by the companies. I don't know how he has been getting copies. He may have made copies partly from our promptbooks and partly from memory of the plays he was in. And he may have been working with others to get texts. Just this year, for example, Danter published an edition of Will Shakespeare's *Romeo and Juliet*, which the Chamberlain's Men didn't authorize. I don't know how Slater could have got hold of that."

"Had you accused him?"

"No. But I think several of our players were suspicious, and he decided it was wise to get out."

"Were he and Tobye good friends? Could Tobye have been working with him?"

"I don't think so. There's no evidence that Tobye was working with printers."

"But Tobye could have found out what Slater was doing?"

"Yes."

"And Slater could have come back to the theatre and killed him to keep him quiet."

"It's possible, but I didn't see anything of Slater after he told Mr. Henslowe he was leaving."

"I think I'll have to see something of him, and soon," Carlin said as he left.

Chapter Eight

❦

Reappearance of a Pistol

CARLIN SPENT another two days questioning members of the Admiral's company without much luck. Towne and Singer and others had shared ale with Tobye in the Mermaid and Mitre, but they had nothing to contribute about his background. He seemed competent and experienced, but he didn't talk much. Nobody admitted any suspicions about Slater or any connections to pirate-printers. Carlin wasn't convinced that the players knew as little as they pretended. Especially, he wasn't sure that John Pig and Wat didn't know more than they admitted. He was increasingly certain that there was something more important here than a squabble among actors. He had his first minor success when he shifted his attention outside the Rose and began talking to the Chamberlain's Men.

Thomas Pope had never met Tobye or Slater, but Will Kempe reported a conversation with Tobye and an interesting meeting. Carlin began the interview with questions about Kempe's interest in the Rose.

"How did you happen to be at the Rose early on the day old Timothy Rudd was killed?"

"I'm always up early, and I like to walk along the Bankside."

"But why go into the Rose?"

"I was going by and heard cries for help and then saw a crowd gathering."

"How did you happen to know young Wat Gayton well enough to vouch for him?"

"I'd seen him around the theatre. He struck me as a harmless young man. I didn't think he should get into any trouble."

"It seems to me you've shown quite a lot of interest in the Admiral's Men recently. What's the reason?"

"I know some of the players. Gadzooks, this is silly stuff. If you'd ask me something sensible, I might be able to help. About that corpse you found, for instance."

"You mean Edward Tobye?"

"That's the only one I've seen recently."

"Did you know Tobye?"

"I talked to him a time or two, and he asked me to meet him at the Mitre the day before he was killed. He was looking for information, he said."

"What about?"

"He wanted to know about *The Isle of Dogs*, why I'd taken the news about it to the Rose and how I'd heard about it. He wanted to know whether I thought it was subversive."

"Did you?"

"I told him I thought some of those dogs ought to be exposed, but I'm not sure he agreed."

"Did you see *The Isle of Dogs*?"

"No. I just heard talk around the theatre."

"What do people say about the play? Who was being criticized?"

"Nobody seems to know. There's talk about a Polish ambassador being one of the most scurrilous dogs, with a whimper instead of a bark."

"Why do you think Tobye was interested?"

"I have no idea. But you might be interested in this. I left before Tobye did, but when I got outside I realized I'd left my hat on a chair near our table. When I returned Tobye had moved. He was sitting at another table. He and a companion had their heads so close together they looked like that two-headed boy in the broadside ballad picture. I recognized his friend."

"Who was it?"

"You'd have recognized him too. Richard Topcliffe."

Carlin would have recognized him. Topcliffe had been in and

out of prison for a dozen years for his activities as a persecutor of
Roman Catholics, not only hunting them down, which was offi-
cially considered legitimate sport, but conducting their punish-
ment, which included torture. He had machines and racked pris-
oners in his own home. One of his successes had been the capture
and torture of the Jesuit poet Robert Southwell, who was executed
in 1595. Topcliffe had been a member of parliament and had nu-
merous supporters even in the Privy Council. He was out of prison,
and supposedly still actively looking for victims, including gypsies
and players or writers critical of government officials, as well as
popish recusants. Most recently, he had written a letter to the
Privy Council calling attention to what he considered subversive
material in *The Isle of Dogs*.

"How do you know Richard Topcliffe?" he asked Kempe.

"I don't know him. But everybody on the Bankside knows who
he is, especially after what he did to Southwell a few years ago."

"Well, let me know if you find out any more about him. I'll
want to talk with you again."

Kempe left. Carlin believed Kempe, and it seemed obvious that
Tobye had been working on the side as some kind of spy. There
was a motive for murder in Tobye's activities, but Carlin had no
good guesses about what the actor was working on or who was
behind him. Topcliffe did enlist followers in his searches, and Tobye
might have been helping him. Topcliffe had been known to pay
spies, and Tobye, according to Henslowe, never seemed short of
funds. It seemed unlikely that Tobye was part of the Essex faction;
it seemed more likely that he was looking for information about
Essex and his followers. Carlin decided he needed help. He went
to see Robert Cecil, who had assigned him to look into the murder.

Cecil was interested. But he said he was puzzled about Tobye's
connections, particularly with Topcliffe. He doubted that he could
be working on his own, without some kind of official or semi-official
authorization. But Tobye was not one of Cecil's many investiga-
tors. And Cecil did not like the idea that Tobye might be working

for someone else on the Council. Topcliffe did have a supporter or two on the Council, who had been active in campaigning against Mary of Scotland, and who still thought there were Catholic conspirators all around, especially among the followers of Essex.

Cecil encouraged Carlin to keep probing. And Carlin went back to the Bankside to look for Topcliffe.

Carlin started at the Mitre. John Page had inherited the Mitre and was one of the most respected vintners on the Bankside. He had no affection for Privy Council agents, but he had always got along well with Carlin, answering his questions without revealing much about his patrons, who sometimes lived a little beyond the law.

"I'm looking for a man who was in here a week or so ago in the afternoon with the player from the Rose who was murdered. He's about sixty-five, thin and tall, with a pinched face. He'd have been well dressed."

Page knew very well whom Carlin was looking for, but he let him continue. "He may have been talking with Tobye, the player who was killed, or with some of the other actors."

"I think you must mean old Topcliffe," Page volunteered. "He comes around here once in a while, hoping to pick up some information he can twist around."

"Do you know where he lives?"

"Everybody knows that. He's riding high these days, since he got out of prison a couple of years ago. He's back chasing Catholics, and he knows how to make a profit out of that. He's got hold of the house of the Jesuit Fitzherbert. All the Fitzherberts have fled to Italy, and Topcliffe's living in the family house, and still looking for someone he can get into a torture chamber."

"You don't seem to care much for Topcliffe."

"He's a scurvy dog, but he's got friends in high places. I think he's got his eye on someone among the players."

"Do you know who?"

"Could be anyone. He doesn't have to have any real evidence. He just likes to watch the rack working."

Carlin wasn't sure what he had learned, but he continued to hang around the Rose, where the Admiral's Men were in the midst of a busy summer. *Jeronimo* remained popular, and Wat became comfortable as Balthazar. The Chapman humors play and *Frederick and Basilea* continued, and Wat got another role at the end of July in a new play, *The Life and Death of Martin Swart*. He saw Anne at least briefly almost every day and was happy as he thought of himself as a real member of the troupe. But he was aware of new tensions in the company since the murder of Tobye, which nobody talked about much but which was on everyone's mind. The Council's investigator, Carlin, was around almost every day, asking especially about Martin Slater, who seemed to have disappeared.

Five days after the murder most of the company were in the tiring house getting ready for a revival of Marlowe's *Doctor Faustus*, which they had not played since January. Alleyn, who had a reputation for his performance in the title role of the old play, was running over lines with Singer, who was playing Mephistopheles. Wat had no part in the play, but he was listening, following Alleyn's speech patterns in his mind. Alleyn stopped as young Tom Downton, handling props, ran in shouting, "Look what I found." He was waving a pistol in the air.

"Where did you get that?" Alleyn asked.

"On a shelf in the prop room, right where it's supposed to be. I'm sure it wasn't there yesterday."

"Did you see anybody around the prop room this morning?"

"Nobody, except actors getting ready for today's play."

"Anybody else see anything?" Alleyn asked.

There was silence.

"Well, we'd better report it to somebody. See if you can raise anybody from the watch." He motioned to Towne who was standing near the door.

As they waited, John Pig pulled Wat aside. "I think I saw Martin Slater in the theatre this morning. Do you think I should tell?"

"Are you sure it was Slater?"

"Pretty sure."

"Then I think you should tell Mr. Alleyn."

Johnny hurried over to Alleyn and got his information to him before Towne returned with Constable Slocum.

"Let's see this gun," he asked. He examined it, smelled it. "Is this the pistol that was missing the other day?"

"I'm sure it is," said young Downton. "I think the rust spots are the same."

"I'd better take this as evidence. Mr. Carlin will want to see it."

Alleyn didn't mention Pig's information to Slocum, but when Carlin showed up an hour or so later he told him that Slater had been seen and possibly had returned the pistol. He mentioned also that he was reasonably sure that Slater had been stealing play scripts. That night Carlin's agents picked up Slater and charged him with attempted murder and murder.

Carlin was back in the theatre a day later to talk to Alleyn, and Wat happened to be in a position to overhear most of the conversation without meaning to eavesdrop, although he moved into the shadows a little closer to them when they started to talk.

"We've found out something," Carlin said, "but Slater insists he didn't kill Tobye or old Rudd. He was on the rack all night, screaming and begging."

"What did you find out?"

"Oh, he was stealing plays all right, and he admits that he slipped in during rehearsal and took that shot at young Gayton. He says he thought it was Tobye in his old role, not Wat. Tobye knew about the play stealing, and Slater just wanted to scare him, to show him he meant it when he told him to keep quiet. He put the gun back thinking somebody in the *Jeronimo* cast would be blamed."

"Do you believe him?"

"I'm not sure, but I think Tobye knew something more important than just some play pirating. Slater ought to be recovered enough by today to take a little more persuasion, but I think he doesn't really know why Tobye was killed. And that's what I want to know. So does the Council."

Wat slipped away and found John Pig in the tiring house.

"I don't think Slater did it," Pig said, after Wat had reported. "He wouldn't use an axe. And I feel sorry for him getting stretched."

"I'm glad it's not me Carlin's got."

"Me too. I know Slater a little. He always needed money, but he never seemed mean."

"But who did do it?"

"It could have been almost anybody, not anybody in the company. If Tobye was into political stuff, it could have been some other agent or somebody from the Chamberlain's Men."

"But Tobye must have been at the Rose for some reason. I don't know who it could be, but I think somebody here thought Tobye was after him."

"You'd better not be walking alone late at night."

Chapter Nine

❦

A Scene Missing from a Shakespeare Play

CARLIN WAS STILL PUZZLING about Martin Slater, but his investigation took a new turn when Robert Cecil summoned him on Privy Council business. Cecil was holding a small book.

"Have you seen this?" he asked.

Carlin picked up the book. He read the title: "The Tragedy of King Richard the Second, as it has been publicly acted by the right honorable the Lord Chamberlain his servants."

"That's the play everybody's been talking about," said Carlin. "I went to see it at the Curtain."

"Did you find it subversive?"

"Well, there is a usurper in it, Bolingbroke, and he forces King Richard to abdicate. People have been likening Bolingbroke to Essex and Richard to the Queen."

"I saw the play two years ago at the home of Sir Edward Hoby in Canon Row. I didn't think much about it at the time, but I can see why people seem to be considering it a political allegory."

"Do you know who wrote the play?"

"The talk around the theatre is that it's by one of the young actors, William Shakespeare. He's done some other plays for the Chamberlain's company."

"What do you know about him?"

"Not much. He had a small part in the play when I saw it. He's been around for a while. Five years ago the playwright Robert Greene talked about him in a pamphlet, and I've heard Will Kempe tease young Will with the words. Greene wrote the pamphlet just before he died of a surfeit of pickled herring and Rhenish wine. He called him an 'upstart crow' and the 'only Shake-scene in a country'."

"I've heard that the young Earl of Southampton has been his friend and sponsor."

"That's interesting," said Carlin, "Southampton is a friend and great admirer of the Earl of Essex. This bears some looking into."

"Do it," said Cecil. I've checked with the Master of the Revels and the Stationers' Register. Shakespeare has some record there. Those long love poems have been reprinted several times, *Venus and Adonis* and *The Rape of Lucrece*."

"I tried reading them once, but my stomach wouldn't take them."

"And this *Richard* quarto was properly approved; apparently the printer bought the copy from the Chamberlain's company."

"It seems to be the usual kind of playbook." Carlin leafed through the pages.

"But there's one thing interesting about it. The book doesn't show anything about Richard giving up his throne. If you saw the play, you remember a scene in which Richard looks in a mirror and talks about the crime of deposing a king. That whole scene is not in the book."

"It's been in the performance."

"Somebody must be worried about the scene. I want you to find out what's going on. You can call the company in for questioning. I'm going to find out some more about this playwright."

The *Richard II* quarto was not the first publication of a play attributed to Shakespeare, as Cecil had found out when he checked the Stationers' Register. Also in 1597 the same printer and stationer who issued the *Richard II* quarto, Valentine Simms and Andrew Wise, had published *Richard III*, another play about English history. Apparently the Chamberlain's Men had also supplied the copy for this edition. The printer John Danter published in 1597 the *Tragedy of Romeo and Juliet*, by Shakespeare, with a badly garbled text, probably from a transcription, perhaps in shorthand taken at a performance. Danter was the printer Alleyn suspected of working with Martin Slater to pirate plays. As early as 1594 there had been quartos of another history play, *Henry VI*, and the tragedy, *Titus Andronicus*. Cecil had heard of *Titus Andronicus* as a play popu-

lar with the groundlings in the theatre because of its violence.
Carlin knew that Will Kempe and Tom Pope had at least attended some meetings of Essex supporters, but he tended to accept their denials of any real involvement. There was always good
wine at those meetings, which may have been the major attraction
for the actors. The cutting of the abdication scene, however, seemed
to him a strong indication that somebody was agreeing with the
widespread rumors that Bolingbroke and Richard could be read as
Essex and Elizabeth. His hopes of uncovering some real conspiracy
revived.

He decided to begin with the printer. Valentine Simms was in
his shop, a neat establishment with two journeymen and two apprentices as well as Simms, all of them busy. One of the journeymen was using the large press, printing folio sheets for a religious
tract. Simms was setting type. He bowed to Carlin, whom he knew
to be an agent of the Privy Council. Carlin went directly to his
questions about the play.

"I'm sure you'll find that everything was proper about the printing," Simms said at once. "Mr. Wise took care of the entry in the
Stationers' Register. The copy was bought from the Chamberlain's
company, the author's foul papers, I think."

"Did you omit one scene from the copy?"

"No, of course not. The play was reprinted as we received it."

"Have you seen the play on the stage?"

"I don't approve of stage plays."

Andrew Wise the stationer distributing the play was at his place
in Paul's Churchyard at the sign of the Angel. Like Simms, he
greeted Carlin with deference, but he knew nothing about any
omissions from the copy that had been given to Simms. He had
not seen the play, but he had heard rumors that the Queen was
not pleased by its theme.

Instead of going to the theatre to interview members of the
Chamberlain's Men, Carlin decided to summon them to a formal
meeting. He sent orders to Richard Burbage, the leading actor of
the company, who had been playing King Richard, specifying that

all sharers of the company, including William Shakespeare, were to appear. Those who appeared, in addition to Burbage and Shakespeare, were Henry Condel, Will Slye, Will Kempe, Tom Pope, John Heminges, and Augustine Philips.

Carlin spoke first to Burbage. "Did you sell the play to Andrew Wise on behalf of the company?"

"I did. We sold two or three plays earlier this year."

"Did you examine the copy before you sent it?"

"Only sketchily. The script had been around for some time, even though we have revived it from time to time. I think the copy was the author's original writing."

"Why did you revive it? Did somebody urge you to play it again?"

"It was always popular. People are interested in history. And I like it."

"Who was the writer?"

"Will Shakespeare here," Burbage pointed him out. "He's written several plays for us."

"Was the scene of Richard's abdication in the copy that went to the printer?"

"I assume so. It was certainly in the copy when Will wrote it. I always played it as it was written."

"You played the part of Richard, did you?"

"That's right. It's a favorite of mine."

"Who played Bolingbroke?"

"John Heminges, usually."

"Did you think you were the hero of the play?" Carlin turned to Heminges.

"No. It's a play about a king. Richard is the hero. The play is a tragedy."

"Is that right?" Carlin turned to Shakespeare.

"It is a tragedy. A tragedy about a king."

"How about that scene that was cut from the printed play? Did you take it out?"

"Of course not. It's the most important scene in the play. Whoever cut it out has no business near plays or a theatre."

"Why would the scene have been removed?"

"I don't know. Discretion is the better part of valor, I've heard. I'm not sure it is."

"Do you mean that the scene is subversive, an attack on the Queen?"

"There is no attack on anybody in the play, except on some of the characters."

"What political purposes did you have in mind when you wrote the play? Were you warning the Queen?"

"I was writing a play. The job of a playwright is not politics. It's to hold a mirror up to nature."

"I remember a mirror in that scene we're talking about. With that mirror the king sees himself as no longer a king. Doesn't that scene give comfort to usurpers and traitors?"

"Not for anybody who understands it. It's about Richard as a man. It's about a king who is more a poet and a dreamer than a practical administrator. We admire him but can't save his kingdom for him."

"Is Bolingbroke a traitor?"

"Perhaps. But some would say that there's such divinity does hedge a king that treason seems impotent. If you remember the end of the play, Bolingbroke is penitent and vows to make a voyage to the Holy Land."

"Why is that important?"

"The play is history. It's all in Holinshed's Chronicle. But I made up the bit about the Holy Land. It shows that Bolingbroke realized his guilt."

"Do you know the Earl of Essex?"

"No," was Shakespeare's answer.

Carlin was not making much progress. He saw no point in questioning Kempe and Pope again, and he doubted that anyone was going to admit cutting the abdication scene. But he turned again to Burbage.

"Has the Earl of Essex seen this play?"

"I have heard that he attended the theatre when it was being performed."

"Why do you think that scene was omitted in the printed copy?"

"Perhaps someone on the Privy Council or in the Office of the Revels ordered it cut. Did you check there?"

"Why would they have wanted it omitted?"

"You know as well as I what the rumors are, that the Queen identifies with Richard and that Essex or his followers are planning some kind of action against the throne."

Carlin suspected that Burbage's guess might well be right. He was also sure that he would not find out any more about it from the Chamberlain's Men, and that none of them were going to admit complicity in any kind of plot.

"If any of you find out more about these matters, I advise you to let me know. I also advise you," he turned to Burbage, "not to perform the Richard play again this year. You may go."

Carlin had still not uncovered the plot he hoped for.

Chapter Ten

❦

A Masked Lady

WAT AND JOHN PIG and Will Barne had all noticed the masked lady who had been coming to the theatre for a day or two, dressed in the latest fashions, accompanied by a footman and a young maid. The Rose often had as many as 2500 people for a new play and had more than a thousand in an average audience. There were always gentlemen and ladies in the boxes and the gallery, but seldom an unaccompanied lady, and seldom one quite so magnificent as this one. The mask, unusual for the theatre, gave her an air of mystery. She seemed interested in the plays and sat quietly alone. The servants discouraged attempts by hopeful gentlemen to join her. She stayed to the end of *Jeronimo*, but left before the end of *An Humorous Day's Mirth*.

"She must be a very great lady," Pig observed as they watched her arrive one afternoon.

"It's a fine coach," Wat noticed.

"How'd you like to get into her bed?" asked Pig.

Wat was embarrassed, but he managed not to show it. "Too soft for me, I bet," he said, but it seemed an interesting idea.

"That dress would make a fine costume," Pig said. "I could use it in Jeronimo."

Doctor Faustus was scheduled again for the next day. Wat was at the theatre at play time even though he had no part. The old play was still popular, and coaches were crowding the street, muddy after a night rain. The pit was filling with a noisy crowd, and Alleyn, already in costume, was hurrying the cast to get started promptly. Wat noticed that the mysterious lone lady was already seated in a box. And then he recognized the lady's maid walking directly toward him. She curtsied as she came up to him, handed him a folded paper, and left without a word. The note was addressed to Wat Gayton. It was unsigned and read simply: "My lady requests that you meet her at her coach after the play."

Wat was both puzzled and impressed. Obviously the lady, whoever she was, was confident enough to assume that Wat had noticed her and could identify her maid. And she knew Wat's name, possibly from his role in *Jeronimo*. But Wat had no guess about why she would want to talk to him. He was excited. He decided not to tell John Pig. Or Anne.

He was outside the theatre well before the end of the play, and had spotted the impressive coach. He waited until the lady had arrived and then approached. She held out her hand but did not remove her mask. Wat took her hand and bowed.

"The coach will be at your dwelling at eight this evening," she said in what seemed to Wat a beautiful low voice. "We know where you live. Please be ready."

She was in the coach with the door closed before Wat could say anything.

John Pig was waiting when Wat came back inside the theatre. "Who is she? What did she look like? What did she say?"

Wat had no answers, but he was beginning to feel excitement as well as confusion as he anticipated the meeting that evening. He told Pig about the appointment for eight, and told him not to mention it to Anne.

"She probably just likes the way you play Balthazar," John said, with obvious irony.

Wat was silent and hurried off to Mrs. Simpkin's. He was not quite sure why he had decided not to mention the lady and the coach to Anne. He knew Mrs. Simpkin and the Captain would be amazed when a coach turned up at the house, but he decided to postpone any attempts at explanation until later. Wat had been experimenting, not very successfully, with a beard, but he shaved carefully after supper and put on his best clothes. The Captain noticed.

"Are you seeing Anne tonight?"

"No, I have theatre business," Wat answered, and went to his room, watching through the window for the appearance of the coach, not entirely sure it would appear. It did appear promptly at eight, accompanied by a crowd of admiring neighborhood children. A footman came to the door asking for Mr. Gayton. Wat followed him with only a "good night" to Mrs. Simpkin and the Captain, who watched open-mouthed as the coach drove off with Wat inside.

It was Wat's first ride in a coach. He looked in awe at the velvet cushions and the gilt trimmings on the windows. Wat knew little of London beyond the Bankside and the places where he and Anne had walked, and the footman and coachman were completely silent as they rode east along the Thames. After about twenty minutes, the coach stopped and the footman motioned Wat toward a door and knocked. A servant opened the door: "My lady is expecting you. Please wait." He returned in a minute or two with the lady from the theatre.

She was no longer masked, and Wat found her clearly the most beautiful creature he had ever seen. She was slim, almost as tall as Wat. Wat was not aware that the glow on her cheeks depended on the new cosmetics that were becoming popular at court, in spite of the Queen's disapproval. She was dressed in bright red velvet, without a farthingale. A white lace ruff framed her long black hair, bound with a gold tiara. Wat, not sure how to behave, decided to kneel, and the lady seemed pleased as well as amused. She caught his hand and raised him to his feet.

"I'm Elizabeth Brydges," she said. "Thank you for coming. I want you to meet some friends."

Wat couldn't think of anything to say.

"I've enjoyed your acting. And I'm sorry I had to be so mysterious. But the Queen doesn't approve our attending the theatre. I hope you didn't mind coming alone in the coach."

"Oh no," Wat said at once. "It was exciting."

"The others are in the drawing room. Won't you come with me."

Three men, obviously gentlemen Wat concluded, and another magnificent lady were seated near a table with wine and food. The men rose as Elizabeth and Wat entered. She led Wat around and introduced him. Wat remembered the name of Mary Fitton. He never distinctly heard the names of two of the men, but the third was familiar. "This, Wat, is Robert Devereux, Earl of Essex. He's been interested in you."

Wat, of course, had heard of Essex, in and out of favor with the Queen, idol of young aspirants to military renown, champion of the Queen in jousting at court celebrations. The tall, handsome courtier, still looking younger than his thirty years, dominated the room, obviously admired by the other two young men as well as by Elizabeth. Wat couldn't find anything to do with his hands and became painfully conscious of the plainness of his dress as he looked at Essex's fashionable long doublet and padded sleeves. He managed to stand stiffly upright and to bow. Essex's friendly manner gradually put him at his ease, and he became almost comfortable.

"I want to talk with you later," Essex said. "But won't you join us in a glass?" Elizabeth steered Wat toward the table and poured a glass of wine for him. Essex turned toward the three men.

"I was given news today that will interest you. You remember the young man with us at Cadiz who was always spouting poetry, John Donne. He's going with us on the Azores expedition."

"Good," said one of the men. "But I thought he was in some kind of trouble about religion."

"That's all cleared up. Old Topcliffe, who hates poets almost as much as he hates Catholics, was hounding him. His brother Henry was put into Newgate long ago as a Catholic, and Topcliffe can't forget it. But I've talked to some people in high places. He's out of trouble."

"I remember him," said another of the men, "but I never could understand his poetry."

"Nor could I," said another. "I remember stuff about catching a falling star, which makes no sense."

"But he was a brave young fellow. I'll be glad to see him again."

Essex walked away, and the three men turned to Wat, who had never heard of a poet named Donne. He was pretty sure that Donne had not written for Henslowe or the other theatres.

"May I get you a pipe?" asked one of the men. "This tobacco is the finest Trinidad, very good for the lungs and the digestion."

Wat was tempted to try it, but he declined, partly because he disliked the smell of the smoke from the men around the table.

The men resumed their conversation, which concerned a new hawk one of them had acquired.

"Are you interested in falconry?" one of them asked Wat.

Wat had known country squires in Tunbridge who had hawks. "I've known some falconers, but I know nothing about training hawks."

"I've acquired a fine young bird," said the new owner. "It was caught wild in the fall in its first year, the best kind to train, I'm told."

"Turberville's book is the thing to follow for the training," said another, referring to the standard guide book to the methods and language of falconry. "You can probably develop it into a haggard."

Wat was not sorry when Elizabeth interrupted and motioned him to a chair beside Essex, who had returned.

"I want to congratulate you on becoming a real actor," Essex said. "Some of my friends in the theatre think you have a great future. Do you know Dick Burbage?"

"I've only seen him play," Wat answered. "He's a fine actor."

"And an important person. You may want to consider moving to the Chamberlain's company one day to work with him."

"Yes," said Wat, "but Mr. Alleyn is a fine man too, and I'm doing well with the Admiral's Men."

"Of course," Essex looked away and hesitated, then turned back to Wat. "You've been having a little excitement at the Rose."

"More than we need," said Wat, "but it hasn't hurt attendance."

"And you've been right in middle of it. Found both bodies and got shot at yourself. I hope you're not in danger."

"Oh, I don't think I have anything to worry about. I don't know anything about what's going on."

"What do you hear about why Tobye was killed?"

"Not much. Some people say he found out something about politics, but I don't know anything about things like that."

"Have you met a man named Will Carlin?"

Wat nodded. "He came to the theatre to question some of us about Tobye?"

"I'd guess he also asked about me." Essex laughed.

Wat smiled uncomfortably and nodded in agreement. "He just asked if I'd heard anyone in the theatre talking about you. I'd heard some talk about your leading an expedition, but I didn't know anything about it."

"Did he ask about a play called *The Isle of Dogs?*"

"Oh yes. Everybody was talking about that. But nobody knew much about it except that a couple of actors were in jail."

One of the young men who had been busy at the table and talking to Elizabeth interrupted. "We need to be on our way. We have more business this evening."

Essex glanced at the fine watch he was wearing on a gold chain. Wat had noticed it earlier and been impressed. He nodded. "Just a few minutes," he said and turned back to Wat.

"These are difficult times, Wat," he said. "There are people plotting against me, and I need to find out all I can. I think Tobye was working for somebody on the Queen's Council who must be my enemy. But I don't know who. And I don't know why Tobye was killed. I want you to keep your eyes and ears open and let me know whenever you hear anything. Elizabeth can get information to me, and you'll hear from her. I think you may know more than you realize. And you may be in danger yourself. So don't say any-

thing to anybody about this meeting, and be careful."
Essex joined his followers. They bowed to Elizabeth. "The coach
will get you home, Wat," Essex said as he left.
Elizabeth joined Wat. "Please stay a little while," she said. "I
need to know you better."
Wat thanked her, and she sat down near him. A gold pomander
was suspended from her girdle, and Wat felt a little giddy from the
perfume. Like all the rest of the evening she seemed unreal.
"You have a happy future in the theatre," she said. "And you
know you're very attractive."
Wat did not know. He had never thought much about the subject. But he was pleased.
"I hope to see much more of you." Elizabeth put her hand on
his arm. "The Earl of Essex doesn't own me, you know, although
he sometimes acts as though he does."
Wat smiled, and didn't know how to answer. Then he did say
what he was thinking. "That would be wonderful."
"I'll call the coach, but you'll hear from me soon. And I'm not
thinking just of any information you may have for Essex."
Mrs. Simpkin and Captain Daglish were both waiting when the
coach dropped Wat, who tried to float past them without a word.
But the captain caught his arm.
"What kind of mischief are you up to, my lad? That's not a
coach from the theatre."
"I'm sorry, but I can't tell you," Wat said, feeling the importance
of Essex's confidences. "But I've had an interesting evening."

Chapter Eleven

❦

"The Count of Exeter's Daughter Knows How to Find Truth"

THE ROSE had no performance scheduled for the next day, and Wat did not make his usual morning appearance at the theatre. He managed with some difficulty to survive the barrage of questions from Mrs. Simpkin and the Captain at breakfast, but he did nothing to satisfy their curiosity. Wat was afraid that Mrs. Simpkin would take the first opportunity to tell Anne about the coach, and for more than one reason Wat was not eager to have Anne questioning him. He kept thinking the whole evening must have been a dream, with the figure of Elizabeth Brydges in the center of it. He felt thoroughly confused, and wanted to talk with someone about what had happened. But he remembered Essex's warning, and he couldn't think where to go for advice. The Captain might have some ideas about Essex, and he could always talk in confidence with John Pig. He thought most seriously of going to Alleyn, but he guessed that Essex might not approve—or that Elizabeth might not. He thought a walk along the Thames might clear his head, which was not accustomed to the amount of wine he had consumed.

Just as he started for the door, there was a knock, and three men appeared. The man in front, obviously in charge, was tall and thin, with wispy gray hair and a sharp nose. He looked very old to Wat, but his voice was firm.

"Are you Wat Gayton, a player at the Rose?"

Wat nodded.

"You're to come with me." And as Wat stepped back he added, "At once."

"Who are you?" Wat asked. He was puzzled but also frightened, wondering whether this summons had anything to do with his adventures of the night.

"I'm Richard Topcliffe, an agent of the Privy Council, commissioned to examine players who may be guilty of lewd and mutinous behavior in connection with seditious performances. You will come at once." Topcliffe took Wat's arm.

And as he did, Captain Daglish, with his sword drawn, stepped in front of Topcliffe. "Take your hands off the lad, you scurvy dog. By Pharoah's foot, he's guilty of no mutinous behavior."

Topcliffe gestured to his two followers, who also drew their swords. "These are Thomas Fowler and Richard Skevington, also servants of the Council, and it's their duty to see that the Council's commands are carried out. Put up your sword."

The Captain backed away with a warning. "By my fackins, if anything happens to this lad, you'll answer to me."

Topcliffe pulled a paper from his pocket. "Here's my authorization. Notice the seal of the Privy Council."

The seal didn't mean much to Wat, but the Captain seemed impressed and stepped aside as Wat followed the three men to a waiting carriage. After a twenty-minute ride they stopped in front of a large house. Skevington and Fowler pushed Wat out of the carriage, and they followed Topcliffe inside and down some stairs to a large room.

"Welcome to my home, young Wat," Topcliffe said with a sneer; Skevington and Fowler laughed.

Wat looked around. The room was damp, with stone floor and walls. There were a couple of benches near one wall with ropes dangling from hooks above them. In the center of the room was a long wood frame, with a roller and crank at each end. Wat had heard of the rack, and he had no desire to be more intimately acquainted with it.

Topcliffe saw him looking at the rack. "That's the Count of Exeter's daughter," he said. "She knows how to find truth."

"I don't know what you want of me," Wat finally was able to say something. "Mr. Alleyn can vouch for me."

Topcliffe laughed. "Tie him up straight, boys. He'll be able to think better that way. Let his toes touch for now. We'll let him see if his memory doesn't get better."

Fowler and Skevington put ropes on Wats wrists and hung them over the heavy hooks. Then they pulled him up so that his toes could just touch the bench below.

"You can be thinking about how God's wrath will be visited on you and other lewd players, instruments of Satan. Plays, where pride reigns and lust flourishes. They tempt apprentices to neglect their duties, and they encourage young boys to dress in women's clothes in defiance of the word of the scriptures."

The three left, and Wat could hear them going up the stairs into the main part of the house.

While Wat was trying to forget the aches in his arms, Captain Daglish and Mrs. Simpkin were thinking about what they could do. The Captain had recognized Topcliffe. He had seen him in taverns and had heard about his activities. He had drawn his sword and run three steps toward the men hurrying Wat to the coach. "I'll cut out your livers, you villainous dogs," he had shouted. And then more practically, "And I'll have the law on you for this."

Topcliffe didn't even turn around. The coach departed.

"I don't like this," the Captain said to Mrs. Simpkin. "We have to do something. This probably has to do with that coach he left in last night."

"I knew he'd get in trouble mixed up with that theatre crowd," Mrs. Simpkin said. "I think I should tell Anne. She knows Mr. Alleyn."

"I'm going to the Rose," Daglish said. "Somebody there will know what to do. That agent who was here from the Privy Council seemed an honest fellow. He may have something to say about this."

Alleyn was at the theatre when Daglish burst in, and he was upset at the Captain's news. He and Joan had developed a genuine interest in the young actor, partly because Joan's friend Anne Page seemed to like him. But Alleyn also was concerned about Topcliffe's agitation against the stage generally, and particularly against the Admiral's Men and the Rose. He had heard about Topcliffe's torture chamber, and he remembered what had happened to the poet Southwell.

"See if you can find Constable Slocum," he said to John Pig, who was listening to the Captain and was concerned for his friend Wat.

Slocum liked to loiter around the theatre, and Pig found him in a few minutes. "Do you have something more about the murders?" he asked Alleyn when he came in.

"Maybe," said Alleyn, "but more important young Wat Gayton who found the bodies is in trouble. Richard Topcliffe and a couple of his ruffians have hauled him off, supposedly to question him. You know what that means."

"That's none of my affair," Slocum shook his head. "Topcliffe has been saying he's an agent for the Privy Council. I have nothing to do with the Queen's men."

"I don't think Topcliffe's really a Council agent. And Wat is no recusant or traitor. You know that after talking to him. You have to come with us to get Wat away before Topcliffe and his thugs really hurt him?"

"It's not in my jurisdiction. Topcliffe's men aren't easily frightened. I don't think you can do anything."

It was at this moment that Will Carlin appeared, still following Robert Cecil's instructions to keep an eye on activities of the players and still interested in Ed Tobye. He heard the news about Wat and was interested, especially because Topcliffe was involved and was apparently claiming some connection with the Privy Council. He saw a chance to find out who was behind Topcliffe.

"Maybe we can do something." he said. "Topcliffe has no authorization to use torture even if he is a legitimate agent. And this may be a chance to find out what he does in that big house of his. Are any of the watch near here, Slocum."

"I have one man outside, armed with a pike."

"I think that's enough, and I think you'd both better come along with us," Carlin said.

"I'm ready to go," Captain Daglish announced loudly.

"This isn't really in my jurisdiction," Slocum was obviously not eager.

"I'm ordering you on the authority of the Privy Council. Go get your man."

Alleyn and John Pig both insisted on accompanying the officers, and Carlin agreed.

"We can get there fastest on the river," Carlin said. "I know the house, and we can be sure that's where they've gone. Go ahead of us and find a waterman," he said to Slocum who had returned with a member of the watch.

In a few minutes they were on the river.

Chapter Twelve

❦

A Taste of the Rack and a Rescue

WAT STOOD for what seemed to him hours, half hanging from the ropes that chafed his wrists. He was fairly sure that he recognized his captor. He remembered seeing the man at the Mitre and hearing that he was called Richard Topcliffe. There was talk about him around the theatre—that he was a Puritan and that he hated actors as instruments of the devil, but none of the players seemed to take him seriously. This, however, looked serious. He wondered if it had something to do with his visit the night before and his talk with Essex. He knew that Essex was not a favorite of the Privy Council, that some of its members were jealous of his intimacy with the Queen. But Topcliffe had no way of knowing about the visit. Wat decided it was best for him to say as little as possible, mainly because he didn't know anything Topcliffe might ask about. He tried not to look at the rack, which Topcliffe called "the Count of Exeter's daughter," but he kept imagining how it would feel.

Topcliffe finally returned, with his two henchmen, and sat down on the straight chair facing Wat. Fowler and Skevington were carrying whips and stood on either side of Wat. "I hope you feel cooperative," he said. "We could shorten those ropes. Now, let's start with who killed Ed Tobye. Somebody has to answer to me for that. Who did you see that morning?"

"Nobody I could recognize," Wat said. "I've already told the Council people that I couldn't clearly see the man. The light was dim, and he was wearing a mask. Tobye was dead when I found him."

"See if you can jog his memory, Tom."

Fowler's whip snapped across Wat's back.

"How about Martin Slater or Will Kempe?"

"No," Will said. "I couldn't see who it was."

Fowler raised his whip again, but Topcliffe lifted a hand to stop him.

"Maybe you hit him yourself," said Topcliffe. "Who ordered you to? Tobye was my man, and I have many enemies among the Rose players."

"He was dead when I found him. Mrs. Simpkin has already told Mr. Carlin that I was at home all night."

"So you talked to Carlin, did you? He's an impostor, you know."

Wat didn't answer.

"What did Slater think you knew when he fired at you during *Jeronimo*?"

"Mr. Carlin says he thought it was Tobye playing his old part."

"You're not helping us much. Those Godless plays always lead to murder and other wickedness. You should think about how you're doing the devil's work and try to tell us which of the players are helping traitors and heretics."

"The players are no traitors or heretics, Mr. Topcliffe. They're good honest men."

"I'm talking about Catholic heretics. I think players are helping a Jesuit traitor. You know the law."

Topcliffe was referring to the series of Parliamentary penal laws passed during the 1580s, exacting severe penalties against Catholics. Anyone caught attending mass could be fined and imprisoned for a year; priests who defied a proclamation ordering their departure were to be ripped open and dismembered by the public executioner. Topcliffe had been zealous in apprehending anyone who could be charged as a Catholic.

"I don't know any Jesuits," Wat said, not quite sure what a Jesuit was.

"I'm looking for one Thomas Southwell. Have you heard of him?"

"Never," said Wat.

"He's the brother of that traitor Robert Southwell, a papist poet who was executed a few years ago. I hear he's pretending to be an actor."

"I never heard of him."

"What were you doing talking to Essex's whore the other night?"

Wat was surprised but also worried. Perhaps this did have something to do with Essex. "I don't know what you mean," he said.

"I think you do. You were seen talking to her."

"If you mean Mistress Brydges, she only told me she liked the play."

"So you were talking to her. What else did she have to say?"

"Nothing," Wat answered.

"I think you can do better than that. Let's try the old persuader, men. Put him on the rack and see if he can remember what that doxie was up to. She knows a thing or two."

The minute Wat's hands were free, he tried to make a run for the door. He was young and quick, and for a minute broke away from Fowler and Skevington. But he still had the ropes on his wrist, and his struggle didn't do much except irritate Topcliffe , who was rubbing his hands at the prospect of watching Wat on the rack. He was smiling as the ropes became taut on Wat's legs and wrists.

"Now we can get somewhere," he said.

As Fowler and Skevington started to crank the rack into action, there was beating on the door, and Wat recognized the voice of Captain Daglish. "Open up in there, or we'll break this door. You've got the navy to deal with, Topcliffe."

"This is private property," Topcliffe answered as he went to the door, drawing his rapier. "Rogues and brawlers have no business here."

"This is the watch," Slocum said more calmly. "We need to talk to you, Topcliffe. Open the door."

Daglish, still brandishing his rapier, was first through the door when Topcliffe opened it, and he rushed to Wat on the rack.

"Stay away from him," Topcliffe said. "He's in my custody, being questioned on orders from the Privy Council. You are interfering in official business and hindering the Lord's work."

"We'll see what's the Lord's work," said Daglish.

"Be calm, Captain" Carlin said, and he motioned to the others to be quiet. "I think you know me, Topcliffe, and I think we know the Privy Council doesn't authorize you to torture honest citizens on the rack. I think I know what Robert Cecil will have to say about this. Now, take the ropes off that young man." He turned to Fowler and Skevington.

Topcliffe was obviously outnumbered, and he was a little frightened at the prospect of Cecil's involvement. He nodded to his henchmen and they hastened to free Wat from the rack. They had already put their whips back on the shelf.

"You may take him," he said. "But there's evil in that theatre, and it should be scourged. I meant the boy no harm. I was only trying to get to the bottom of the knavery that has twice led to murder."

The Captain and John Pig helped Wat to his feet, and they all left.

Topcliffe went on talking, partly to his henchmen, partly to himself. "This is not the end. Those scurvy players need to understand what evil they're fostering. I've seen that young boy John Pig wearing women's clothes, flouting the word of God. Those houses of the devil should all be pulled down and some time good citizens will do it."

Wat was confused as the wherrry moved them swiftly on the Thames back to the Rose. He still could think of nothing he had heard or seen that related to the murders. He had found the bodies by chance and had seen nobody until after he had called for help. But everybody seemed to think he should know more. The Captain quizzed him, asking about other members of the company, especially Towne and Tom Hearne, who had only recently joined the company. Then Carlin followed him into the theatre to ask about his adventure with Topcliffe.

"Did he ask about the Earl of Essex?" Carlin began.

"Yes," Wat said, "but I couldn't tell him anything." Wat decided not to mention his interview with Essex or Topcliffe's question about Elizabeth Brydges.

"What else did he ask about?"

"Mostly he wanted to know about Ed Tobye. He said that Tobye was his man and somebody would have to answer to him for his death."

Carlin was obviously interested in this. "Do you think he meant that he was paying Tobye? What else did he say about him?"

"He didn't say anything else about Tobye. He did ask about somebody else I never heard of, somebody named Southwell."

"A poet named Southwell was executed a few years ago, and Topcliffe had a lot to do with his conviction. Why did he bring him up?"

"He said he was looking for his brother. He said the brother might be an actor."

"Did he say any more about him?"

"Nothing. That's when he put me on the rack and you and the Captain came in. He just said again that he had the authority of the Privy Council."

"That's interesting."

"He had a letter from the Council, he told me, and was ordered to question me to find out about traitors."

Carlin nodded and left. He needed to talk to Cecil, who would be interested to know that Topcliffe was claiming to be an agent of the Privy Council.

Wat hadn't seen Anne since his escape from Topcliffe, although she had visited Mrs. Simpkin and asked about him. Wat wasn't sure what he would say to Anne, especially about meeting Essex and Elizabeth Brydges, whom he couldn't get out of his thoughts He had never met anybody like Elizabeth, and he was flattered by her interest in his role in the play and her attention to him in the London apartment. It had been his first ride in a private coach. His second ride was in Topcliffe's hired coach.

The next morning Wat's back reminded him sharply of Fowler's whip, and he gave up his habit of an early arrival at the theatre. He was still being pampered by Mrs. Simpkin with a late breakfart when Anne arrived, presumably on an errand from her mother.

"Mrs. Alleyn told me what happened. Are you all right, Wat? I've been worried."

"Oh, I'm fine."

"But you should see his back where the whip caught him," Mrs. Simpkin said, and Wat was pleased at Anne's look of concern."

"And he was about to get a real taste of Topcliffe's methods when we arrived." Captain Daglish had come in when he heard Anne's voice.

"I'm glad you got there before they started with the rack," Wat said. "I don't know what I could have told them, and I wasn't feeling very brave."

"It's a good thing he didn't know about that coach last night." said the Captain. "You might have been in more trouble."

Wat didn't answer, but he noticed that Anne had heard. As usual he walked with Anne back to the Mitre. She pleased him by showing her concern again and urging him to be careful. But Wat was sure she would ask about the coach, and he was not sure how much he should tell her. He remembered Essex's insistence that he not mention his visit, although he didn't know why it should be a secret. Anne finally asked, "What did the Captain mean about a coach?"

"Oh, it was just theatre business." Wat couldn't think of any way to improve on his earlier lie. "A man sent his coach to take me to a meeting with some people interested in the *Jeronimo* play. It was a fine coach."

"Why would it have interested Topcliffe?"

"I don't think it would. That was just the Captain's imagination."

"I've heard Topcliffe doesn't like players," Anne said.

"I think that's right. I hear he's a Puritan, and I think he just hoped I'd say something about the other actors that he could use."

Anne took his hand before she left him when they reached the Mitre. "I was so worried about you, Wat." Wat put his arm around her awkwardly and kissed her for the first time.

He walked off toward the Rose, feeling very happy, but also a little guilty about his obviously implausible explanation of the coach. He was also aware of how frequently the image of Elizabeth Brydges popped into his mind.

John Pig was waiting for him at the theatre. "Mr. Alleyn's worried about you," he said. "Why is old Topcliffe after you?"

"I don't know. He thinks I know something about Tobye, I guess. I found out Tobye was working for Topcliffe. He was some kind of spy."

"Maybe he found out something."

"I think so, but I don't know what."

"I've heard that Topcliffe is mainly looking for Catholics he can feed to those machines in his house," said Pig. "Those impressed me, and you were about to find out how they work."

"I'm glad you all got there before they started cranking. Do you know any Catholics Tobye might have been after?"

"No. But Topcliffe is interested in the Earl of Essex too, and there's talk that some of the Chamberlain's Men have been a little chummy with the Essex crowd."

"Maybe that's why Carlin and the other Council people keep asking me about Will Kempe."

"And one of them could have sneaked in here and whacked Tobye if he was nosing around the theatre at night."

Wat was beginning to get new ideas about why Topcliffe had decided he was worth questioning. Apparently the question about Elizabeth Brydges meant something. Someone in the theatre must have told Topcliffe about his meeting with Elizabeth after the play, and Topcliffe might have found out about his meeting with Essex. Wat had no desire to get mixed up in any kind of plot nor in any of the alleged ambitions of the Earl of Essex. But he did keep thinking of Elizabeth.

Chapter Thirteen

🍂

𝔄 𝔏𝔢𝔰𝔰𝔬𝔫 𝔦𝔫 𝔏𝔬𝔳𝔢

BOTH KYD'S OLD PLAY *Jeronimo* and the new Chapman play that Henslowe called *A Comedy of Umers* remained popular, and Wat was comfortable in his roles. Tobye's death and the departure of Slater also left vacancies in other casts, and Wat picked up new roles in *The Witch of Islington* and *Captain Thomas Stukeley*. Wat was busy with the new parts and regular performances, and he managed almost to forget about Topcliffe and Essex and Tobye. On the fourth day after his visit to Topcliffe, however, he was met as he was about to enter the Rose by the man he remembered as a servant of Elizabeth. He handed him a note and then stepped back as Wat read it:

> "I should very much like to see you this evening. The coach is not available, but you can easily get here by water. If you can come, my man will meet you at the theatre at eight and show you the way to the apartment. Please let my man know whether he should meet you.
>
> Elizabeth Brydges"

Wat was puzzled. He had decided that it would be wisest to have no more to do with Elizabeth Brydges or anyone connected with the Earl of Essex. He was also pleased and flattered by the invitation.

Elizabeth's servant bowed. "Do you have a message?"

Wat had decided to decline the invitation; nevertheless he said after little hesitation, "Please tell Mistress Brydges that I accept. I'll meet you here at eight."

The messenger bowed again and went off toward the river.
Wat didn't understand why he had accepted. He decided he would
be outside the theatre at eight and would explain that he couldn't
go along. But he was curious about why Elizabeth wanted to see
him. Essex was off chasing Spaniards, according to the talk around
the Rose, and Wat had been warned about getting too friendly
with the group of zealots who were supposed to be plotting all
sorts of dangerous activities. On the other hand, there was the
possibility that Elizabeth needed his help for something; Wat could
imagine various ways in which he might save her from wicked
relatives or offensive suitors. With Essex out of the city she might
be vulnerable. Or she might need help in getting away from Essex,
a possibility that intrigued Wat. He could decide later whether to
go. There was a performance in the afternoon.

Wat forgot a line in the last act of *Jeronimo*, and John Pig had to
cover for him.

"You seem to be dreaming instead of acting today," Pig said as
they walked away from the theatre. "How about stopping in at the
Mitre? Maybe your old friend Topcliffe will be there?"

"That's not very likely," Wat said. "I don't think he wants to see
any of the Admiral's Men in a hurry. Anyway I have to get home
and work on some lines for tomorrow."

He tried to slip off to his room when he reached Mrs. Simpkin's,
but the Captain called to him as he started up the stairs.

"I saw Topcliffe and his two henchmen today," he said. "They
were walking around outside the Curtain. I was tempted to teach
him a lesson for what he did to you the other day, but it didn't
seem a good time."

"I don't think he'll be after me again," Wat said. "He's after
bigger fish."

"Well, I'm watching for him. And you let me know if he tries
anything again."

Wat stayed in his room until Mrs. Simpkin called him for din-
ner.

The Captain noticed that Wat had changed his clothes. "Are

you expecting that coach again?" he asked, with a leer.

Wat laughed, not entirely convincingly. "No, but I do have to go back to the Rose. I'll be back later tonight."

"Are you seeing Anne?" Mrs. Simpkins asked.

"I won't have time tonight." And Wat hurried off to meet Elizabeth's man and explain why he couldn't go with him.

He was early for the eight-o'clock appointment, and he took his time walking along the Thames, listening to the watermen talking to each other as they went along. By the time he reached the meeting place outside the Rose, he had forgotten his resolve to refuse Elizabeth's invitation. She might even be in some trouble.

Elizabeth's servant was waiting, leaning against a post and chewing on what looked like a straw, as if he hadn't entirely forgotten growing up in the country. He raised his cap when he saw Wat, but didn't say a word and didn't smile when Wat greeted him. Then he motioned toward the river. "We could walk," he said, "but a boat is easier. I'll call a waterman."

"Is it far?" Wat asked.

"We'll be there soon."

"Would you tell me your name?" Wat asked.

"Jem."

They found an available boat at once. Wat made some attempts at conversation, but got only monosyllables as responses. Jem gave the waterman directions to stop, and led Wat along a narrow path to the big house Wat remembered, surrounded by tall oaks, dark except for a brightly lighted room on the first floor to the right of the main entrance. Jem turned away from the main door to a smaller entrance away from the lighted room and tapped on the door. It was opened a crack until someone inside recognized Jem. A maid whom Wat remembered from his first visit then opened the door. Jem walked away and Wat entered. He followed the maid and her candle to the room Wat remembered, where he had first met Elizabeth. Elizabeth was alone, seated on a sofa, wearing the elaborate red velvet gown Wat had been seeing in his fantasies. The maid left, and Wat walked to Elizabeth. She gave him her hand.

"It's good of you to come. I hope coming without the coach wasn't too difficult. I thought it might seem strange for the coach to turn up again at Mrs. Simpkin's."

"It was no trouble. Jem managed very well."

Elizabeth rose and filled two glasses. "Essex is off looking for Spaniards. Some of his hangers-on are meeting downstairs, but they aren't allowed in this part of the house."

"I noticed the lights."

"They have all sorts of plans, but I pay no attention to them. I see you're in a new play. Do you like it?"

"Oh, very much," Wat answered.

"I'll come to see you. I enjoyed your Balthazar."

"Thank you."

"And I've been wanting to see you again. I hope you don't think me forward for asking you."

Wat couldn't think of any answer. He was still a little dazed just from looking at Elizabeth and wondering how he came to be there.

"But also I want to warn you. I don't know what Essex told you the other night, but it's dangerous to get mixed up with his followers. Some of them are rash and headstrong and have ambitious plans. If they've seen you here, they may think you're trying to find out what they're doing. Especially since that man Topcliffe questioned you. I heard about that, and I've been worried. Topcliffe has spies everywhere. I know he's been watching some of the players. Somebody must think you know something, and I don't want you to get into trouble."

"I don't know anything about plots or conspiracies. Old Topcliffe did question me, but I couldn't tell him anything."

Elizabeth filled their glasses.

"He probably thinks you know something about the player Tobye who was killed. Tobye was one of Topcliffe's spies."

"Yes, one of Topcliffe's men said that."

"Topcliffe probably has other spies in the theatre. Some of Essex's men think he does and think you know about them. They've told me to find out what you know."

"I wish I had something to tell you."

"I just want you to be careful. I heard that someone shot at you during a rehearsal."

"I think that was just a mistake. An actor named Slater admitted firing the shot; he didn't know I had taken over Tobye's role in the play."

"Anyway, let's not worry about these things tonight. I really just wanted to see you again."

"I wanted to see you too," Wat managed to say.

"Let's just have a quiet evening by ourselves. But excuse me for a minute. I'll be right back. Fill your glass. That's sack that Essex brought from Cadiz."

The sack was excellent, and Wat did fill his glass again. He walked around the room, partly hoping to ease his nervousness. A fine tapestry on the wall opposite the sofa seemed to be a picture of Paris walking out of the sea with a naked Helen in his arms. The other walls were bare. Heavy drapes covered windows on the wall behind the sofa. Wat was half eager and half afraid as he waited for Elizabeth to return. He was acutely aware of his lack of sophistication and experience with ladies like Elizabeth, and for a moment he considered slipping out the door and back to the security of Mrs. Simpkin's. He had dismissed the notion before Elizabeth returned, still in red but in a long loose gown with her hair unbound over her shoulders.

"Do you like this better?" she asked. "I feel much more comfortable." She sat down and motioned for Wat to sit beside her.

"You're beautiful." Wat surprised himself by blurting out what he was thinking.

"I'm glad you think so." They were both quiet for a minute. Elizabeth took his hand. "You're a very attractive young man."

Wat felt his face flushing red, but he also began feeling bolder, with distinct stirrings in his modest codpiece. He pressed Elizabeth's hand. She moved slowly, and her robe slipped from her shoulders, showing just the start of the curve of her breasts.

Elizabeth repeated, "You're very attractive, Wat," and she slowly unbuttoned and pulled off his doublet, then pulled his head toward her and kissed him. Wat was no longer thinking about what was going on or what he should do, and somehow his clothes came off and Elizabeth's gown fell on the floor and he found himself with her on the bed. It was Wat's first experience, but with Elizabeth's expert guidance all went well. Wat drifted in a kind of dream, feeling Elizabeth's body as he moved into her, sensing her reaction to his excitement, not thinking of where he was or why he was there. And then they were lying quietly and Wat drifted off to sleep.

He woke with Elizabeth gently shaking his shoulder. She was sitting beside him, wearing the crimson gown, smiling at Wat's sudden awareness of his nakedness. She kissed him gently on the lips and handed him a cup of the sack they had been drinking. Wat felt a quick return of excitement, and reached out to draw Elizabeth to him again, but she laughed and pulled away.

"You were wonderful, Wat," she said, "but it's late. The men down below are getting noisy. They may be planning something. You must go."

"Will I see you again? Soon?"

"You'll hear from me."

Wat pulled on his hose and doublet and sipped at the sack. He was still far from reality, but he managed to get dressed and think about getting home.

"You remember how to get back on the river," Elizabeth said, seeming eager to get him on his way. "I'll let you out a back door and you won't be seen."

"May I come again? Tomorrow? Now that I know how to get here."

"You must not come unless I send for you. Remember what I told you about being careful. I think you should not tell anyone about your being here." She was guiding him down a dark hallway.

Chapter Fourteen

❦

A Girl and an Ambush

WAT FOUND HIMSELF with a closed door behind him, facing the path toward the river. He was thinking of Elizabeth's dark hair falling over her shoulders and of the whiteness of her breasts. Suddenly he was aware of loud talk coming from the lighted room he had noticed earlier. He heard a door open and heard three or four men shouting farewells. One of them announced that they'd be waiting at the Mitre Tavern, presumably to be joined by others from the room. The light through the open door was bright enough that Wat could get a good look at four men as they moved out toward the path. He thought of Elizabeth's warnings and had an impulse to run, but instead he slipped behind a tree and waited for them to pass. He returned quickly to reality as he recognized John Singer and Thomas Towne of the Admiral's company as two of the men.

They moved noisily toward the river, and Wat could hear them calling for a waterman and then moving up the Thames. He followed quietly and found a boatman; he could keep the four from the Essex house in sight as his boat moved along the Bankside, and he watched them leave the river at the steps near the Rose. He waited at the steps until they had turned toward the Rose and the Mitre and then followed, keeping out of sight when he could. Actually he was in no danger of being observed; the wine from the earlier meeting and anticipation of what the Mitre could offer preoccupied the four men.

Wat didn't want to go into the Mitre, even though the four would have no reason to know he had seen them earlier. But there was a chance that Anne or her father might see him, and he wanted to avoid any meeting. He wasn't sure why he had followed, but he was curious about how Towne and Singer were involved and interested in who might show up to meet them. He moved into the shadows at the side of the old building and discovered a spot where he could look through a window at Singer and Towne without much danger of being discovered. He couldn't hear what was going on, but obviously the four had much to discuss.

Wat watched for about half an hour, and had just about decided to leave when three other men joined the group he was watching. Wat recognized Will Kempe at once, and he was fairly sure that another was Thomas Pope, who also played clown parts with the Chamberlain's Men. He wondered if they also had been in the brightly-lighted room at the Essex house. He remembered Carlin's questions about Kempe and his concern about the play on Richard II that the Chamberlain's Men had been offering.

The talk in the tavern went on, and the ale flowed, but Wat was increasingly bored. Just as he turned to leave, however, someone grabbed his arm and pulled him back into the shadows. He pulled away, frightened.

"Wait a minute, Wat," a voice said. "I mean no harm."

In the dim light Wat could see only a shadowy figure, bent over and apparently crippled somehow.

"Don't you know me?" the voice went on. "I've had a bad time. I'm Martin. Martin Slater. They've had me on the rack, but they finally let me go."

Wat could hardly recognize the actor, who had obviously been beaten, but he said, "I'm sorry Martin. I didn't recognize you."

"They turned me loose, but I'm supposed to watch people, especially players, and help them find traitors or heretics. And I'm supposed to watch you."

"Why me?"

"They think you must know more than you've said about Tobye's murder or about the Essex people. And they know I was the one who shot over your head in the theatre. I thought you were Tobye. I was only trying to scare him, but they don't believe me."

"But I don't know anything about those murders."

"They think Topcliffe must have found out that you know something, or he wouldn't have questioned you."

"Were you working for Topcliffe the way Tobye was?"

Slater seemed not to hear the question. "I just want to warn you.
I'm sorry about that shot. You need to be careful. I'm a dead man."

"What do you mean?"

"They'll get me the way they got Tobye. I'm too weak to get out
of London. But I'll be hard to find."

"Who'll get you? Do you know who killed Tobye?"

"There are papists around, and Tobye was looking for them. He
must have found the heretic Topcliffe wants. It's a player, you can
be sure. Tobye must have identified him."

Slater limped off into the darkness before Wat could ask him
anything more. Wat decided he wasn't likely to learn anything
more at the Mitre. He turned back toward the Rose and his way
back to Mrs. Simpkin's. He felt ready for bed. There was no sign of
Slater. The night was dark; there was no moon, and Wat hurried,
feeling a little apprehensive, partly because of his meeting with
Slater.

He was about half way home when he heard what sounded like
someone crying, and he saw a figure just off the path in a little
alcove near the river. He stopped and could see in the dim light
that a girl was standing there, crying softly. She looked completely
naked. She motioned to him and he heard a soft call which sounded
like "Wat." He moved toward her, curious and a little frightened.
This night he had seen his first nude woman; it was hard to realize
he was seeing his second so soon. For a moment he had a notion
that this might be Elizabeth, although he could not see enough to
recognize anybody.

He heard again, "Wat, come closer." She drew him into the
alcove, Wat had never seen her before. Then suddenly she burst
into laughter and ran away, throwing on the robe she had been
clutching. And Wat saw two men in his path with drawn rapiers,
blocking his way from the alcove. One of them looked familiar; he

was almost sure he was one of those he had seen at the Essex house. He stopped. They didn't say a word, but moved slowly and menacingly toward him. There was no way of retreating from the corner into which the girl had drawn him. The men continued to come closer; Wat thought there were smiles behind their beards.

"I think young clever boy needs a lesson." one said softly.

"He's not so clever, if you ask me," said the other.

"But he needs to learn his place. Don't you want to know why you're in trouble?" The first man leered at Wat and flourished his sword.

"You don't seem to know where it's proper for you to be paying visits. We think you need a lesson."

Wat was terrified. His throat was so dry he couldn't have answered if he had wanted to. The swords almost touched him. Suddenly, almost without thinking, Wat sprang between the two blades and the two men and raced down the path. He felt a sharp pain in his arm as one of the swords caught him, but he didn't notice the blood until he realized that he had escaped and no one was following him. He stopped to catch his breath. He washed his arm hastily in the culvert beside the path, pulled his sleeve tight to slow the bleeding, and hurried on to Mrs. Simpkin's. He discovered that the wound was only a deep scratch and found cloths to fashion a rough bandage. He fell into bed, where he lay awake trying to make sense of his confusion.

Obviously Carlin of the Privy Council had been right in his suspicions that some of the players were among the followers of the Earl of Essex. Wat had heard talk about plots against the Queen presumably for the purpose of elevating Essex to power; but Essex had not looked like a traitor when Wat met him. And now he was off on some kind of military expedition, supposedly commissioned by the Queen. Topcliffe and his spies were apparently looking for any kind of activity they could call subversive, but they also were concerned about Essex, just as Carlin was. Carlin apparently had no love for Topcliffe. Both Topcliffe and Carlin wanted to find out who had murdered Tobye, and they seemed to think Wat knew something about it. He was puzzled about the two who had way-laid him and the girl who had drawn him into a corner. He was fairly sure that one of them was from the Essex group. They must have seen him leaving Elizabeth's apartment. They might have thought Elizaeth had given him dangerous information or that he had gone there hoping to spy on the group's plans. They might have assumed that Elizabeth belonged to Essex and Wat was tres-passing. Or they might have seen him talking to Slater, who apparently had been trying to get information about Essex.

How did Elizabeth fit into all this? She was living in a house that belonged to Essex, and Wat had to believe that she was Essex's mistress, as Topcliffe had labeled her. Wat's fantasies created vari-ous pressures forcing Elizabeth into dependence on Essex, and cast himself in various roles in which he carried her off to some romantic paradise. He was still too much under the spell of Elizabeth's eyes to suspect any ulterior reasons for her show of affection. He was not sure how to interpret her warnings. Was he to be careful that none of Essex's friends connected him with Eliza-beth. Or was he to be careful not to get involved with Essex's men, or not to seem to be one of them. Elizabeth had learned from someone that Topcliffe had questioned Wat. Wat wished he could talk to somebody like Alleyn or John Singer, and then he remem-bered that Singer had been one of the group at Essex's house. Per-haps he could talk to the Captain or John Pig without mentioning Elizabeth, but that might not be easy, especially since John had seen her at the theatre.

Wat finally went to sleep. He woke early and tried to slip out without talking to anybody, but Mrs. Simpkin caught him and immediately noticed the bandage.

"What has happened to you, boy? Let me have a look at that arm." She loosened the bandage and pulled Wat to a chair.

"You can't go off this way. How ever did you manage a cut like that?" She brought water and clean cloths and set about washing the wound and putting on a clean bandage.

"It was the armor I wear when I play Balthazar. It's old, made in

Germany, and the corselet has split leaving a sharp edge. I was careless and scratched my arm. It's nothing." Actually the old armor did have a split, and Wat's fabrication had some plausibility.

"I might have known. No good ever comes from those playhouses. Now you have something to eat before you go off to the theatre."

Captain Daglish appeared as Mrs. Simpkin worked on the bandage and immediately was interested in the wound.

"That's a bad scratch," he said. "It doesn't look to me like a break in the armor could do that. It must have been pretty sharp."

"It was."

"It looks to me like the kind of thing a rapier could do, especially if whoever was using it didn't know his business very well."

Wat didn't answer. He finished his breakfast and then walked for nearly an hour before he got to the Rose, where he learned that Martin Slater had been stabbed to death during the night outside the Mitre tavern.

Chapter Fifteen

❦

Old Armor Doesn't Bite

WAT HAD NO ROLE in the day's play, Ben Jonson's comedy, *A Tale of a Tub*, in which John Singer had made a reputation as a clown using an exaggerated Yorkshire dialect. Wat hadn't seen the performance, and he wanted to watch, partly to see how Singer played the part. Most of the members of the company were around, getting ready for the afternoon performance or working on parts for other plays. Henslowe was in his office talking with Alleyn, and Towne and Singer were checking costumes. Most of the talk was about Slater's murder.

"I wonder what those thugs of Topcliffe were doing last night," said Towne, "Fowler and Skevington."

"Wasn't Slater working for Topcliffe?" Singer asked. "Didn't Topcliffe tell you that when he questioned you, Wat?"

"He told me about Tobye." Wat remembered that Slater hadn't answered when he asked him about working for Topcliffe. But he was sure that Slater's fear had something to do with Topcliffe's group. He thought he should tell somebody about his meeting with Slater and Slater's fear of being killed, but he didn't want to get more involved than he already was. He remembered the two swordsmen and glanced at the bandage on his arm.

"Somebody thought he knew something," Towne said, "but Carlin had him on the rack for hours and must have found out anything he knew about Tobye."

John Pig, wearing a new gown that he was trying on for the afternoon performance, came up to Wat. "What happened to your arm?"

"I scratched it on that old armor I've been using in *Jeronimo*, and Mrs. Simpkin thought she should put a bandage on it. It's nothing, really."

Towne and Singer turned and noticed the bandage. "You're not going in for sword play, are you Wat?" Towne said. "That can be dangerous."

Wat laughed. "I only fight with old German armor. I was checking over the corselet I wear in Jeronimo. It developed a split in the last performance, and I caught my arm on a sharp edge."

"I was hoping you'd fought a duel over John Page's young daughter," Singer put in. "She's a pretty package."

"Duels are not for me," Wat said.

"You better take care of that arm, anyway," Pig said. "Cuts like that can be dangerous. Does Anne know about it?"

"No, I haven't seen her today. It's not worth worrying about."

Sergeant Philip Slocum walked into the theatre just in time to hear Wat's words and notice the bandaged arm. "Good morning, young Wat," he said. "I see you got into some kind of trouble last night? Were you up at the Mitre, by any chance?"

"No, I wasn't in the Mitre," Wat said, trying not to emphasize the *in*.

"How did you get the wound in your arm?"

Wat decided to stick with the armor story, even though he was afraid nobody believed it.

"Where is this armor that attacked you?" Slocum asked, obviously skeptical.

"It's in the property room. I was looking at it to see if it might be repaired before the next performance of *Jeronimo*. I didn't realize the sharp edge was there."

"Let's go look at it," Slocum said.

Wat found the split corselet with no trouble, but Slocum seemed unimpressed by the strip of metal that was protruding.

"It doesn't look very dangerous to me," he said. "When did you get the cut?"

"Last night."

"What were you doing here last night?" Slocum asked, but went on without waiting for an answer. "How well did you know Martin Slater? You know somebody killed him last night."

"Not very well. He left the Rose some time ago."

"You knew he took a shot at you during one of the plays?"

"I've been told he was the one. But he thought I was somebody else."

Slocum turned to the others. "Which of you were at the Mitre last night?"

Nobody answered.

"I've talked to John Page," Slocum said. "I know you were there." He pointed to Singer and Towne. "Who else?"

Nobody said anything.

"How about you, Hearne?" Slocum said, "Somebody saw you there."

Hearne didn't answer.

"I saw old Topcliffe and a couple of his men there," Towne said. "Have you questioned him?"

"We'll get to him," Slocum said. "Did you talk to those players from the Curtain who were there?" he asked Towne.

"I talked to Will Kempe and Tom Pope."

"About what?"

"About plays. They wanted to know about Ben Jonson's play. They thought Jonson was supposed to be writing for the Chamberlain's Men."

"What did they have to say about the Earl of Essex?"

"About what?" Singer showed great surprise. "Why would we talk about Essex?"

"Don't be smart with me. I know what the Queen thought about that King Richard play."

Slocum used that as a parting shot, and left with no further questions.

John Pig pulled Wat aside. "How did you get your arm hurt?"

"I told you," Wat said.

"I know better than that story. I've seen that break in the corselet. It wouldn't scratch your bottom if you sat on it. Did it have anything to do with the lady in the carriage? I thought she might lead to trouble."

"No," Wat said. "Nothing." But he then told Pig about his adventure on his way home.

"Was the girl really naked?" Pig sounded envious. "Could you see what she looked like?"

"I could see. She didn't have a stitch on. But I'd never seen her before, even with clothes on."

"Did you recognize the men? Were they Topcliffe's?"

"I'm sure I'd seen one of them before, but not at Topcliffe's. I think he's one of the followers of the Earl of Essex."

"Somebody thinks you know something or maybe thinks you shouldn't be talking to ladies who come to the theatre in a coach. You've got to be careful. Mr. Alleyn's worried about what's going on, and so is Mr. Henslowe."

"I'm being careful."

Wat walked away. He realized that what he most wanted was to see Anne and talk with her. He was feeling guilty about his night with Elizabeth, even though he was constantly thinking of how soon he could see her again. He was not thinking of any confession, but he thought that Anne might somehow make him feel better, even less confused. He walked up toward the Mitre, hoping he might find her.

What he found was a scene of considerable confusion just outside the inn, near the spot where he and Martin Slater had talked the night before. He recognized Carlin, the agent from the Queen's Council, who was supervising several men looking in the bushes beside the path. Some of the usual patrons of the tavern were outside, looking at the blood on the spot where Slater had been found and recounting what they knew of the discovery of the body. Wat managed to slip by without being recognized. He spotted Anne helping her mother and signaled to her without going inside. Wat caught her arm as she came out and pulled her away from the door.

"Could you get away and come for a walk with me?" Wat asked.

"What's happened to your arm, Wat? Are you hurt?"

"No, it's just a scratch. I want to tell you about it. Can you come?"

"In a minute."

Anne went back inside, and Wat could see her talking to her mother. She threw off her apron and joined Wat again.

"I've been worried about you. I haven't seen you for a week. And your arm?"

"I've missed you. And I need to tell you about my arm. A lot of things have been happening."

They walked away from the tavern, avoiding the people still milling about the murder scene. Wat took her hand. "I don't know what's going on, but some men attacked me last night on my way home. That's how I hurt my arm."

Wat reported on his adventure, leaving out the girl decoy, describing his escape with adequate modesty but in enough detail to insure Anne's sympathy.

"You might have been killed," she said. "What did they want? Why did they stop you?"

"I don't know, but there's something else I need to tell you. I haven't told anybody, but I saw Martin Slater last night. It must have been just before he was killed."

Wat told her about Slater's appearance in the dark, still suffering from his experiences on the rack and afraid he would be killed. "I never really knew Slater, but he seemed to think I could help him somehow."

"Do you think that had anything to do with the men who attacked you?"

"I don't know. I'm all mixed up. I don't know anything about these murders, but everybody seems to think I do."

Wat wanted to tell her about seeing Singer and Towne leaving Essex's house, but he wanted to avoid mentioning his visits there. "Everybody asks me about the Earl of Essex." He thought she might have heard talk about Essex and the players.

"Mr. Alleyn said something about Essex and some of the Chamberlain's Men. But I don't know what he meant. I think you should tell Mr. Alleyn about all this. Maybe he can help. Or maybe Mr. Henslowe can."

"I don't want to get in trouble. And if I tell about talking with Slater, they may think I murdered him. I don't know what to do."

"Do you think Topcliffe or his men were after you? They could have seen you with Slater and thought he told you something that could damage one of them."

"I didn't recognize any of Topcliffe's men, but I'd seen one of the men before."

"I have to go back and help my mother," Anne said. "But please go talk to Mr. Alleyn. He'll help you decide what to do."

"Can we meet again after the play this afternoon?"

"I have to take some things to Mrs. Simpkin. You could meet me there."

He left Anne at the door of the tavern. He felt a little better, in spite of his guilt feelings about Elizabeth, and decided he would go directly back to the Rose and talk to Mr. Alleyn. He had taken only about a dozen steps away from the door when he felt a hand on his arm. Will Carlin was smiling pleasantly. "Could I have a word with you, Wat?"

Chapter Sixteen

Fabrications and Skepticism

WILL CARLIN was still looking for subversion or treason, and he was still convinced that something significant was behind the murders and might give him a chance to rise in favor with the Privy Council and the Queen. But he had been frustrated in most of his investigation. The questioning of Slater had yielded almost nothing, except some information about Topcliffe that Carlin already had. But Slater had aroused Carlin's interest with his repeated insistence that he "was a dead man." Carlin could get no explanation except Slater's comment that "the Catholics and traitors" were still after him. Carlin doubted that Slater really knew who was after him, but he must have been getting close. Carlin was sure that some of the Chamberlain's Men were friendly with the Essex crowd, but he hadn't been able to get anything but jokes from Will Kempe and Thomas Pope. His spies had turned up very little that seemed important, until he got a report that young Wat Gayton had been seen coming out of Elizabeth Brydge's apartment. Carlin didn't know quite what to make of this, but he found it interesting. There was no shortage among Carlin's informants of allegations about Elizabeth, mostly unfounded gossip based partly on the jealousy of other women connected with the court. Her connection with Essex was well known, but there were also rumors about her interests in the theatre, particularly in the male players. According to one rumor, Elizabeth had helped recruit some of the actors to join the young zealots who were supposedly working on a conspiracy to put Essex on the throne. Carlin thought that Essex knew better than to push such plans himself; he was too confident in his role as Queen's favorite. But many of his supporters were both rash and ambitious, and Carlin suspected that among them he might find candidates for charges of treason and perhaps also murder.

He had trouble figuring out Topcliffe's interest in the players at the Curtain and the Rose, especially his attention to Wat. He had been unable to discover who on the Privy Council was sponsoring Topcliffe. Cecil, he thought, probably just didn't know. Topcliffe's main activity had always been exposing and persecuting Catholics, and Carlin was unaware of any rumors of heresy connected with the followers of Essex. Both Tobye and Slater, Carlin now knew, were being paid by Topcliffe for information. They might have threatened some kind of disclosure or wanted more money and become dangerous enough to Topcliffe that they had to be removed. Carlin thought that unlikely. It seemed more likely that Tobye and Slater had been successful enough in some of their prying to make them candidates for elimination. Old Timothy Rudd had probably just happened to see or hear something compromising to somebody, but Carlin realized that he knew almost nothing about Rudd. He made a mental note to have one of his agents investigate the old man's background. All of which made Carlin more sure that the answer to his questions as well as the discovery that might improve his fortunes was in the theatre, the Curtain or the Rose or both.

He doubted that young Wat was involved in any kind of conspiracy; but he had discovered the first two bodies, he had been shot at by Martin Slater, and apparently he now had something to do with Elizabeth Brydges.

"Another of your fellow actors seems to have run into trouble," Carlin began. "How well did you know Slater?"

"Not well," said Wat. "He'd been playing in the country before he came to Mr. Henslowe."

"When did you last talk to him?"

Wat was not ready to tell Carlin of his meeting with Slater just before his death, and he partly avoided the question. "He was dismissed just about the time Tobye was killed. Apparently he was stealing play scripts for printers."

"He confessed to shooting at you. You knew that?"

"Yes, I heard that, but apparently he thought he was trying to scare Tobye, not to shoot me."

"Where were you last night about midnight?"

"I was at home, at Mrs. Simpkin's."

Wat could tell from Carlin's expression that he had made a mistake. Carlin confirmed.

"One of my agents reports that he saw you leaving the apartment of Mistress Elizabeth Brydges last night, not long before midnight."

"He must have made a mistake," said Wat making another mistake.

"Do you know Elizabeth Brydges?"

"I don't think so. Does she come to the theatre?"

"Often, I'm told. But you don't know her?"

"I see many women who come into the theatre, but I don't recognize this name."

Carlin's smile was skeptical, but he didn't press. "I'll have to talk with my agent again. When did you find out about Slater's death?"

"When I came into the theatre this morning. Everybody was talking about it."

"Have you hurt your arm?" Carlin pointed to the bandage.

"I got a deep scratch from a rough edge on the armor I've been wearing in *Jeronimo*."

Wat realized that Carlin didn't believe this any more than Slocum had, but he couldn't think of a better story.

"Will it keep you from acting?"

"No, it's only a scratch. It bled a little so my landlady bandaged it."

Again, Carlin didn't press. "Do you have any idea who might have murdered Slater?"

"No. I heard that he had stolen some play scripts for printers, and I suppose he might have got into trouble that way. But nobody in the company would have resorted to murder over something like that."

"Do you remember the trouble about a play called *The Isle of Dogs* at the Swan? Did Slater have anything to do with that?"

"I don't know."

"Do you know an actor named Gabriel Spencer?"

"I've heard that he has been in the Marshalsea. But I don't know him."

Carlin was silent for a few seconds, looking into the distance. Obviously the young actor was lying, and Carlin was not sure why. But he was experienced enough as an investigator to know the value of patience. He turned to Wat. "I'll talk to you again. You might think again about where you were last night."

Wat's immediate reaction was an urge to leave at once for Tunbridge, far away from the variety of problems he faced. He was frightened. He realized that he had made a series of mistakes in the interview with Carlin. He knew that the two men who had waylaid him were serious. He had been lucky when his rash move succeeded; he could not count on such luck another time. He was also confused. He didn't know whether he should talk to Alleyn or how much he should tell him if he did. He was especially reluctant to say anything about Elizabeth, partly because he couldn't face not seeing her again. Obviously some people, apparently including Carlin, knew that he had seen Elizabeth. And although Wat was not even slightly sophisticated about women, he was aware that Elizabeth's interest in him might not be based exclusively on his attractiveness in bed or his acting ability. His ego wouldn't allow him to think that Elizabeth's demonstrations of passion were anything but sincere, but he couldn't forget that she had arranged for him to meet Essex. He couldn't guess whether telling about his meeting with Slater would do anything to help solve his murder. But he decided he would talk to Alleyn.

He found Alleyn in Henslowe's office.

"I've been hoping you'd come in," Alleyn said. "Young Anne thinks you're in some kind of trouble."

"I may be." And Wat told Alleyn about the attack and his cut arm and also about the warnings from Slater.

"According to Slater, then, you're being suspected by both the Council agents and Topcliffe's gang who think you have some information about the Essex group and also about the murders?"

"I guess so. But I really don't know anything." Wat was thinking that apparently he was also in trouble with at least two of the Essex faction, but he didn't mention that.

"Do you know what Slater meant when he said he was a dead man? Who was after him?"

"He just talked about papists."

"Did he think that some of the players are Catholics? Or some of Essex's followers?"

"He thought Tobye must have found out something about a player. If Carlin told Slater to watch me, he wouldn't have been afraid of Carlin's men."

"I wonder if you've told me everything. I don't see why you should be suspected of working for Essex. Have you been especially friendly with any of the Chamberlain's company? They're under suspicion because of that play about King Richard."

"I hardly know any of them. I've met Will Kempe and Pope."

"Well, you need to be careful, Wat. You're getting to be a good actor, and I hope you don't spoil your chances by getting mixed up in politics."

"I'm not interested in those things."

"Somebody seems to think you are. Or that you know things you aren't telling. Be careful walking home at night."

Wat was aware that Alleyn, like Carlin, seemed skeptical as well as puzzled, but he still thought he had to protect Elizabeth from any embarrassment. He thanked Alleyn for advice and went into the tiring house to get ready for the afternoon performance of Chapman's humors play. He was thinking mostly of Elizabeth.

Chapter Seventeen

❦

A Confrontation at the Theatre

CARLIN was also thinking of Elizabeth. He had never seen her, but he had heard stories of her beauty. He knew that she was not a favorite of the Queen, that she had been accused of various indiscretions around the court. And, above all, he knew that she was the mistress of Essex and was reputedly very much involved in any of the political plans of Essex or his followers. She was quite capable of trying to enlist Wat as a kind of spy in the theatre. And Wat seemed innocent enough of political intrigue to be useful to Essex without knowing it.

He doubted that he would get much more from Wat about his meeting with Elizabeth, but it occurred to him that Wat might have confided in his closest friend John Pig. He approached Pig on his next visit to the Rose.

"I hear you and young Wat have been taking an interest in the ladies in the boxes at the Rose," Carlin began.

Pig was embarrassed, not sure what Carlin knew. "I don't know what you mean," he said.

"Haven't you been interested in Elizabeth Brydges? She comes to the theatre in a fine coach and has her maid with her. I think you talked to her at least."

"No, I never talked to the lady. Wat and I admired the coach, but I never knew the lady's name."

"Somebody heard you make a remark about how you'd like to take her to bed, isn't that true?"

"I may have said something like that." Pig wondered who had heard him. "She was very attractive. But I never talked to her."

"Did Wat?"

"I don't know.

"Are you sure? Didn't Wat tell you about meeting her?"

"He may have mentioned something about it."

Carlin pressed and managed to extract all Pig knew about Wat's exploit with Elizabeth, which was not much but confirmed what his agents had reported. He dismissed Pig, but he was fairly sure that Wat's cut arm was related to his visit to Elizabeth.

Pig went looking for Wat immediately, and didn't find him at the theatre. He walked to Mrs. Simpkin's, and didn't find him there either. But he did find Anne, who had come on an errand to Mrs. Simpkin and was lingering on the chance that Wat might appear.

"I'm glad to see you, Anne," John said. "I'm looking for Wat. Carlin, the Council agent, has been asking me questions about him."

Anne Page was a quiet, modest girl, better educated than most middle-class girls. The notion that education was only for boys, was changing under the influence of Queen Elizabeth, who was proud of her Latin and her writing ability. Anne had learned some Latin, partly from a curate, friend of her father. She had read Sir Philip Sidney's *Arcadia* and other popular fiction. She could sew and help with the cooking, and could play a little on her father's lute and carry her part in a madrigal. She had never had much reason to assert herself, to do anything beyond her chores around the Mitre and her errands for her mother, many of them to Mrs. Simpkin. But she found herself feeling compelled toward some kind of action. Wat was the first man in whom she'd had any interest, and their walks and other adventures opened a new world for her. She had never consciously examined her feelings for Wat, but she was aware that she was worried about his safety after his escape from the ambush. She also was aware that she was lengthening her errands to Mrs. Simpkin hoping that Wat would appear.

"I'm looking for him, too," she confessed to Johnny Pig. "I haven't seen him for a day or two."

"Carlin seems to think he may be in trouble."

"I think so too. Somebody obviously considers Wat a threat. I wish he'd be more careful."

"Did he tell you anything about the two men who attacked him? I think he recognized one of them."

"He didn't tell me who they were. Do you know anything about a coach? Captain Daglish asked Wat about a coach, suggested that it was connected with the two men."

Pig guessed why Wat hadn't told Anne about the coach, but he thought she probably ought to know about it.

"A fine lady has been coming to the theatre in a coach, and one day she sent her servant to ask Wat to meet her. She had seen him in *Jeronimo*. Wat talked to her after the play, and she gave him a note, making an appointment for that night. She sent the coach for him that night, and Wat went to meet her."

"What happened?"

"I don't know. The next day I asked him about the coach and the lady, but he said he couldn't talk about it. I never heard any more."

"Did he tell you the lady's name?"

"No. But from something Carlin said I think her name is Elizabeth Brydges. Wat never told me her name."

"Has she been back at the Rose?"

"I haven't seen her."

"If she comes again, would you tell me. If you have time to come get me, I'd like to see that coach."

"I'll try," Pig said. They both left without finding Wat.

Anne wasn't sure why she wanted to see the coach or the lady in it, but she was thinking more and more seriously that she ought to be doing something to help Wat. She thought of talking to her father, but didn't want to reveal how seriously she was thinking of the young man. She did talk to Joan Alleyn, who knew that Wat and Anne were together with increasing frequency. Joan had heard of Elizabeth Brydges.

"She's out of favor in the court, partly because rumor has it that she's the mistress of the Earl of Essex, who's a favorite of the Queen, at least some of the time. The Queen likes to keep a tight rein on her ladies in waiting, and she could be a little jealous. If Wat's mixed up with her in any way, he does need to be careful."

"Does Elizabeth Brydges come to plays?" Anne asked.

"I've never seen her. But there is a rumor that she's interested in one or more of the players. I don't know which ones."

Anne left Joan determined to try to find that coach. She had no notion what she could do if she found it, but she was sure that the coach was connected with whatever threatened Wat. She did not quite admit to herself that she felt a proprietary interest in Wat and wanted to assess her competition. She was not going to turn Wat over to a fine lady without a struggle.

Two days later, Pig came running to the Mitre to tell her that she had her chance.

"The lady and the coach are at the Rose," he announced. "Wat is in the performance today. The maid took a note to someone, but I couldn't see who. It couldn't have been Wat; he's on stage. The coach is still there."

Actually faced with the opportunity, Anne was frightened, but she took a deep breath. "Let's hurry, Johnny. I want to get there before she leaves."

"The play won't be over for another hour, but she sometimes leaves before the end."

"Then we'll hurry. Will Wat still be busy?"

"He won't be able to leave till the play is over."

The coach was still there, with the coachman and a footman. Anne sent Pig back to the theatre, saying she wanted to look longer at the coach and would stay outside.

She was not sure what she intended to do, but she had decided that she had to speak to Elizabeth. She was rehearsing possible approaches, not very happy with any of them.

She had been waiting only a few minutes when she saw the footman and the coachman suddenly pull themselves up to stand at attention, and then she noticed that the lady had indeed left before the end of the play and was approaching the coach, accom panied by her maid. She was masked. Anne was awed by the fine clothes, the red farthingale and the wide ruff. She couldn't move for a minute, but then she found herself hurrying toward the coach, determined to speak.

She reached the coach just as Elizabeth did, stepped in front of Elizabeth and curtsied very low. "My lady," she said very softly. "May I speak with you?"

Elizabeth turned to her maid, about to have the intruder sent away. Then she changed her mind. "What is it, child?" she asked.

"Please, my lady, it's about a friend of mine."

"And what have I to do with a friend of yours?"

"It's about Wat, Wat Gayton."

"So, you're a friend of young Wat." Elizabeth laughed softly.

"Yes, if it please your ladyship."

"I have met young Wat. I admired his Balthazar. I've been helping him a bit with his education. I think he may be developing some new tastes and new interests." Elizabeth looked pointedly at Anne's modest dress.

Anne was more angry than embarrassed, but she couldn't think of anything to say.

Elizabeth laughed again. "And what is it you want me to do about Wat?"

The laughter angered Anne still more, and she gained a little courage. "I think he's in trouble. Two men tried to kill him the other night, and I think it had something to do with you or your coach or your friends. I want you to stop whatever is threatening him."

What is your name? Elizabeth asked.

"Anne. Anne Page."

"And do you know Wat well?"

"We are friends."

"What makes you think I have anything to do with Wat's safety."

"I know he was in your coach. And after that he was attacked."

"My dear young lady, I don't know who is threatening your young man. But Wat's a big boy." Elizabeth paused and smiled.

"A very big boy. He can probably take care of himself."

"I think his trouble has something to do with you."

"Wat is a good actor and a handsome lad. And he's not half bad in bed. I wonder if you know that."

Anne felt her cheeks turning red, but she went on more pointedly. "Perhaps the Earl of Essex or some of his friends think Wat should not have seen you."

"I think you'd be wise not to speculate about such things. I sent for Wat, and he enjoyed our evening; my friends didn't know about it. But I'm afraid I'll have to give him up. I hear he's been finding bodies all around the theatre. I have too many important connections to get mixed up with that sort of thing."

Anne was relieved by this news, which was perhaps all she had hoped for from Elizabeth. But she persisted. "Wat knows nothing about those murders. I'm worried about his safety."

"I have nothing to do with his safety. I find him quite interesting as young men go. But I can't answer for every ruffian that may be associated with the Earl of Essex. And I don't know what Wat's got mixed up with. Old Topcliffe is dangerous. I advise you both not to get involved in any of his business. Topcliffe has already talked with Wat, and he might want to talk to you. He likes questioning young girls."

Anne couldn't think of anything to say. She thought of delivering a sharp kick to Elizabeth's shin or tearing off the red farthingale.

"If you're really interested in young Wat, I suggest you not reproach him for his fling with me. He didn't have a chance. Get him into bed yourself as soon as you can. You'll be pleased."

Elizabeth turned and stepped into the coach. She waved as the coach pulled away.

Anne was relieved at Elizabeth's assurance that she was finished with Wat, and she was intrigued as well as embarrassed by Elizabeth's advice. But mainly she was angry, both at Elizabeth's arrogance and condescension and at Wat's faithlessness. She had no idea of how much Wat might be deceiving her. Was he involved in the murders? What had Topcliffe suspected? Why had two men attacked him, and what did they have to do with Elizabeth? She decided not to tell him about her meeting with Elizabeth, but she also knew she did not want to see him.

When Wat returned to Mrs. Simpkin's that evening, he found a note from Anne. It was brief:

"Since you prefer the company of a lady of the court, I prefer not to see you again. I cannot tolerate deception."

Chapter Eighteen

❦

A Different Elizabeth

THE NOTE UPSET WAT and also confused him. He was puzzled about how Anne had found out about Elizabeth, and he could only guess about how much she knew. But it was obvious that she was hurt and angry. Mrs. Simpkin sensed that something was wrong, although Anne had not commented when she left the note. She greeted Wat at breakfast with a question.

"What have you done to that girl?" she asked.

"Nothing that I know of. But I guess she's upset."

"She was very quiet when she came today. Does this have something to do with that coach the other night?"

"That coach didn't mean anything."

"I hope you're not getting in too deep with that theatre crowd."

Captain Daglish had also seen Anne bring the note, and he added his comments. "Anne's a fine girl, and she must be worried about what's going on. She knows about old Topcliffe."

"I don't have anything to do with whatever Topcliffe is concerned about. I'm just trying to be a good actor."

"Anyway, somebody's pretty handy with an axe around that theatre. And Anne looks worried to me. You'd better try to see her and straighten things out."

Wat agreed, and he was determined to try to talk to Anne as soon as he finished in the theatre, in spite of the firm words in her note. He was, however, indulging in a good deal of elaborate rationalization. He was, on the one hand, telling himself that Anne's anger was not serious and probably temporary. She probably knew no more about his excursions down the river than that he had been seen talking to a lady in the theatre. Explaining that there was nothing serious between him and Elizabeth, that she was only interested in his acting, should mend matters at once.

On the other hand, he was justifying his eagerness to see Elizabeth as a need to discuss Carlin's questions with her—totally unrelated to the recurring image in his mind of Elizabeth sitting on her bed with her scarlet gown falling off her shoulders. Wat was hoping for a summons from Elizabeth, rationalizing that he had to see her before Carlin interviewed him again. He was fairly sure that Carlin had information at least about the trip in the coach, and apparently one of Carlin's spies had seen him leaving the apartment. He told himself that he needed to protect Elizabeth's reputation—and he was naive enough to believe it.

When he got to the theatre he learned from John Pig that Elizabeth had been at the theatre the day he was playing in Chapman's humors play. He was puzzled by Pig's report that Elizabeth's maid had been seen carrying a message to somebody, obviously to somebody else. Pig did not mention that Anne had met with Elizabeth.

As soon as he could leave the theatre, Wat walked to the Mitre, hoping to see Anne. She was not there, and Wat got a clear impression from her mother that she would not see him even when she returned from an errand. He easily decided that his explanation to Anne could wait and that he had to see Elizabeth in spite of her express orders that he should not come without a summons. He had to warn her about Carlin's agents and also get her advice about what he should tell Carlin.

At eight that evening, the time of his earlier meetings, he set out on the Thames on the route he now knew. As on his previous visits, there seemed to be a meeting of some kind in a brightly-lighted wing on the ground floor and a dim light in Elizabeth's apartment. Wat's courage was waning as he reached the door, but after a minute's hesitation he knocked. He waited, but there was no answer. He pushed the door and it swung open. The hall inside was completely dark, but Wat knew his way, and he could see a crack of light under the door of the room where he had been with Elizabeth the last time. He moved cautiously toward it. He couldn't hear a sound. He knocked gently and thought he could hear movement inside. He knocked again, but there was still no sound; and after a couple of minutes, Wat pushed the door. It was unlocked. He saw a man with an armful of clothes slip out the side door near the bed. He was sure he recognized him. Elizabeth, quite naked, was sitting on the edge of the bed staring at him.

"Who are you? And what are you doing here?" Elizabeth shouted, reaching for the scarlet dressing gown Wat remembered.

"It's Wat. I had to see you."

"You young idiot. I told you never to come here without an invitation."

"I thought you'd like to see me."

"I like to see you when I invite you. This is a grownup world around here, no place for young fools. Don't get the idea that I'm constantly riggish, just waiting around to take you to bed whenever you feel like it. One night doesn't include a permanent invitation." Elizabeth pulled the red gown tight around her, and suddenly seemed to Wat less beautiful than he remembered.

"But I need to talk to you."

"All right. But don't think that you can burst in here and expect me to like it. I have my own life and no time for reckless boys. The man you saw leave is not going to forget this, and he probably recognized you."

"Who was he?"

"An old friend, who knows how to be discreet when it's necessary."

"I think it was John Singer, of the Admiral's Men."

"If you think so, you'd be wise to forget it. And forget you saw anybody."

"I've been careful. I haven't told anybody about being here or about meeting the Earl of Essex. But that's what I need to talk to you about."

"It's better you not tell anybody."

"But I think Will Carlin knows. He's an agent for the Privy Council."

"What have you to do with Will Carlin? He's Robert Cecil's man and no friend of Essex or any of us. You should stay away from him."

"I'd like to, but he's investigating the murders at the Rose, and he thinks I know something about them. He thinks the murders have something to do with Essex or his followers, and he keeps asking me what I know about Essex."

"What have you told him?"

"Nothing. But his spies are around, and I'm pretty sure he knows about my being here. He asked about your coach."

"Knowing me won't help you any. I'm not a favorite of the Queen these days. You can tell him you talked to me about the theatre, that I asked you about Balthazar."

"I did. I think he didn't believe me. Something's going on, and I don't understand what." Wat told her about being waylaid by two swordsmen.

"Probably they were sent by Carlin. Or maybe old Topcliffe was responsible."

"I don't think so," Wat said. I think I saw one of them here earlier that night."

"If you've been talking to Will Carlin, some of the people here may think you're a spy. And coming out here tonight won't change their minds."

"But Essex asked me to be on the lookout for people working against him."

"Yes, that's why he wanted me to bring you here. But now it doesn't seem a very good idea. We didn't know you were going to get mixed up in another murder."

"Essex wanted you to invite me?"

"Of course. At least the first time. I wasn't just being a stage-struck female. But the second time was my idea, and I won't deny that I enjoyed having you. You're a very attractive young man, and I wish I could keep you. But it won't work."

Wat had no comment.

"If you have to admit to Carlin that you were here, it probably won't make any difference. But the more you get mixed up in these affairs, the more you may be in trouble. I suggest you forget about ever being here and pay more attention to that attractive young Anne Page. She might develop into quite an interesting person. You'd better go now, and be sure nobody is following you."

Wat slipped quietly out the door, trying to adjust to his new feelings about Elizabeth and wondering how she knew about Anne. It was dark, but he thought he caught a glimpse of Singer, now with his clothes on, going into the lighted room he had noticed when he came to the house. He thought for a second about following, finding out what was going on, but he quickly gave up that notion and started on the path to the river, where he was fairly sure to find a boatman.

He had gone only a few yards when he thought he heard sounds of someone following him. He quickened his pace, but the sounds become louder. He started to run, stumbling on the rough path in the dark, and then he tripped on a tree root and fell heavily to the ground. When he got up he found himself facing two men with drawn rapiers. One of them held a burning torch, and in its light Wat recognized one of the men who had waylaid him on his way home from the theatre. The other man grabbed Wat's arm.

"We're not going to use these tonight," he said, flourishing his rapier. "John Singer says you're harmless."

"But we're here to warn you," the other man said. We met you when the Earl was here, and we know he talked to you about giving him information. Now that seems a bad idea. Especially it seems a bad idea for you to be turning up in Mistress Brydge's apartment."

Wat couldn't think of anything to say. He did manage to pull away from the hand on his arm.

"You're to stay far away from this place," the man continued, "And you're not to tell Will Carlin about anything you've seen here. Now get on your way, and watch where you step."

The two men disappeared. Wat moved on toward the river, limping a little in deference to a bruise on his left knee. He found a boatman at once and slipped into Mrs. Simpkin's without seeing anybody.

Chapter Nineteen

❦

Suspects in the Theatre

WAT DID NOT SLEEP WELL, but his fantasies about Elizabeth were different. He was dreaming more about her connections with political plots than about her white breasts. And he was feeling a combination of guilt and affection as he thought of Anne. He now thought Anne was probably seriously angry. She must know more about his visits to Elizabeth than he had thought. Explaining did not seem so easy. He thought again of returning to the quiet of Tunbridge. Then he remembered the excitement of the plays, of Alleyn's comment that he was becoming a good actor, and the chances for new roles in the plays Henslowe was acquiring. He thought about Anne. He knew he had to stay in London.

He also realized that he was in trouble. Carlin certainly suspected him of some connection with the Essex faction, and everybody was aware of Carlin's ambition and his concern to expose anything that could be considered subversive activity. Topcliffe and his spies were equally zealous. Wat could be pretty sure that they both knew of his visits to Elizabeth and suspected that he was somehow involved in the maneuvers of the Essex group. Carlin could even suspect him of the murders. Wat wasn't happy at the thought of either Carlin's or Topcliffe's rack.

He remembered also the warning as he left Elizabeth's apartment from two of Essex's henchmen, as well as the warnings from Elizabeth herself. He was puzzled about Singer's connection with the Essex group, although his relation with Elizabeth seemed clear. For the moment, Singer seemed to have reassured at least some of the Essex faction that Wat was not a spy.

One possibility was to go to Carlin and tell him everything he had held back, his meeting with Slater and his visits to Elizabeth and Essex. He was no longer worried about Elizabeth's reputation. But both the two who had followed him and Elizabeth, had warned him against talking to Carlin, and Wat had no reason to think that Carlin would believe him after his earlier fabrications. Carlin seemed to think that he might remember something more about whoever had run out of the theatre after Tobye's murder. Wat had tried.

As he considered different courses of action, he decided that the only way he could really solve all his problems was to find the murderer. Almost any of the Admiral's men could have committed all three crimes, as could a number of outsiders. Singer and Towne were certainly friendly with some of the followers of Essex. He knew they had been at the Mitre at the time he had seen Slater, and they could have been there when he was killed. Elizabeth had referred to Singer as an old friend, apparently an old lover. Either Singer or Towne might have a motive if any of the victims had discovered that they had some connection with a treasonous plot. Tobye and Slater obviously had been spies of some sort.

Carlin suspected Will Kempe and Tom Pope of the Chamberlain's Men, presumably because they had been seen with friends of Essex and were involved in the play about Richard II. But they had no more to do with the play than other members of the company, including Richard Burbage. Old Topcliffe was certainly capable of murder, and Wat would have been happy to discover that he was the guilty one. But he doubted that Topcliffe had been faking when he said that Tobye was his man and vowed to make the murderer pay.

Carlin seemed to think that he might remember something more about whoever had knocked him down after Tobye's murder. Wat had gone over and over the incident but couldn't think of any clues to identification. There was also the question of how Towne and Singer fitted in. Wat had seen them leaving Essex's house, but he had trouble thinking of either Singer or Towne as a murderer. Wat wasn't sure why Carlin suspected Will Kempe and Tom Pope of the Chamberlain's Men. He had heard talk about Gabriel Spencer of Pembroke's Men, who had killed a man the year before, someone named James Peake, who had attacked Spencer with a copper candlestick. But Spencer hadn't been around since the *Isle of Dogs* affair. John Pig seemed to think that Tom Hearne was a suspicious character, and nobody seemed to know anything about him. And Timothy Rudd had been murdered before Hearne joined the Admiral's Men.

Captain Daglish was waiting for Wat when he came down for breakfast, later than usual after his restless night.

"Well, Wat," he said, "maybe you won't be finding any more bodies. Constable Slocum caught a cutpurse at the Bear Garden yesterday, and he thinks he's the Rose murderer."

"Why does he think so?" Wat was not ready to rely much on Slocum's insights.

"The man's a rogue, and he's been seen around the Rose. They'll make him talk. How's your arm?"

"It's fine."

"But the two that cut you are still out there. You need to learn to use a sword or a pistol I'm ready to give you lessons. I can make a soldier of you. And you need to know how to use a rapier for the theatre. Some of the actors are so bad they'd be killed in a minute in a real fight."

"Thanks. I'll try to learn. But I have to get to the theatre now."

Most of the players were around the tiring house when Wat arrived at the Rose, reviewing parts and checking costumes for the afternoon. Scheduled was the second performance of the new play, *The Life and Death of Martin Swart*, in which Wat had been given a part. He saw John Singer talking with Towne and Tom Hearne and Ed Juby, and he tried to walk away to avoid talking to him. He was fairly sure that Singer had seen him at Elizabeth's or that Elizabeth had told Singer about Wat, perhaps asked him to vouch for Wat with Essex's men. He thought Singer might be embarrassed about his very informal departure from Elizabeth. But Singer called to him.

"Wat, can I talk to you a minute?"

Wat turned and waited. He had decided not to mention seeing Singer the night before.

"You gave me a turn last night," Singer said, showing no embarrassment at all. "If I'd known who you were, I wouldn't have run off. I got cold before I got my clothes back on. You're playing in pretty fast company."

"I'm sorry I interrupted," Wat said, surprised by Singer's openness.

"I hear you've been tupping Singer's dark-eyed ewe," Towne put in. "You're getting ambitious."

"You don't want to get mixed up with that crowd or with the Brydges woman," Singer said. "They can be trouble."

Singer gave Wat a kind of paternal pat on the shoulder and turned back to the other players.

Wat was completely baffled by Singer's attitude. He had assumed that both he and Towne would want to conceal any relations with Essex's people. He realized also that his exploit in Elizabeth's bedroom was not a secret around the theatre, and he suspected that he was in more trouble with Anne than he had thought. Apparently Elizabeth Brydges was fairly well known to some of the actors, especially Singer, and Anne might have learned something about her from Joan Alleyn. He understood, perhaps for the first time, how much Anne meant to him. He had trouble shifting his attention to the afternoon performance and his new part. He was glad to notice that Will Carlin was not around the theatre.

Chapter Twenty

❦

Carlin's Trap

CARLIN HAD NOT BEEN in the theatre since the time he had
questioned the players about Slater's murder, but he had not
been inactive. He was, in fact, feeling optimistic about what he
had found out and the possibility that he might uncover a serious
plot. He was sure now that Towne and Singer and Wat Gayton
had all been with the Essex people on more than one occasion. He
knew that all three of them had been around the Mitre tavern the
night Slater was killed. He was aware that Wat's story about scratch-
ing his arm on old armor was fiction; and he had identified one of
the two men who had attacked him, a member of the Essex faction. He didn't see any reason for doing anything about the two.
They apparently were either thinking of Wat as a spy or resenting
his attentions to Elizabeth, but he thought they were not an important part of any large conspiracy. He knew that both Tobye and
Slater had been connected with Topcliffe and his search for Catholics or other subversives, and he thought he might profit most
from trying to find out what they had discovered.

More interestingly he had picked up information about old Timothy Rudd that seemed to lead in new directions. Rudd, he learned,
had been a handy man around the theatre for only about three
years. Before that he had been friendly with both Richard Topcliffe
and Topcliffe's man, Richard Skevington, and had been mentioned
in court records as the main accuser in 1592 of the poet Robert
Southwell. Southwell had come to England in 1589 and avoided
prosecution under the new anti-Catholic laws until Rudd discovered him celebrating mass and informed Topcliffe. There was no
mention of Rudd in connection with Southwell after 1592, but he

had apparently worked with Topcliffe, who was the leading enthu-
siast in the three years of imprisonment and torture before the
poet's execution in 1595. Rudd, Carlin now knew, was not just a
nice old man who had picked up some dangerous information. He
fitted with the other victims. All three of them were associates of
Topcliffe, all potentially dangerous to somebody whom they were
investigating.

Carlin decided that he was ready to start more serious questioning. The murderer seemed certainly to be one of the players in
either the Chamberlain's or the Admiral's company. No one else
had so much opportunity. And the obvious motive seemed to be
that Topcliffe's agents had turned up evidence that either threatened the success of a plot or, more likely, could support charges of
treason against some actor. It was time to press for answers, maybe
even to try Topcliffe's methods of persuasion.

Carlin started the next day. Towne and Singer readily admitted
that they had visited friends in the Essex faction, but they denied
any interest in possible plots against the Queen. Singer admitted
visits to Elizabeth Brydges, but pointed out that they were anything but political. Will Kempe and Tom Pope denied that Essex
had anything to do with the Richard play, and Carlin found no
reason to connect them with any plot. He spent more time with
Tom Hearne, whom he had not questioned before. He pressed
hard to get information about Hearne's activities before he joined
the Admiral's Men.

"How long have you been earning your living as an actor?"

"About ten years. I started with one of the companies in the
country."

"Were you acting before you joined the company here?"

"I've been with a company on the continent for almost three
years."

"Where?"

"Germany mostly."

"Are any of the players who were with you here now?"

"I don't think so."

Carlin decided to talk with Henslowe about actors in Germany. He was not satisfied with Hearne's answers. Then he found Wat again.

"I've found out a few things since the last time we talked. Maybe you have some better answers for me."

Wat nodded. "I guess you know about the cut on my arm."

"I know. Did you recognize the men who attacked you?"

"I think I had seen one of them at the Earl of Essex's house."

"Do you know Essex?"

"I just talked with him a few minutes one night. He was leaving on an expedition."

"Have you thought any more about the man who hit you and then ran out of the theatre after Tobye's murder?"

"I've thought, but I couldn't see him clearly and his mask covered his face."

"How big was he? Did he walk like Singer or Towne or any of the other actors?"

Wat had thought often about the man who had apparently killed Tobye, but couldn't associate him with anyone he knew. He was too heavy for Singer. He might have been Towne or Tom Pope, but Wat hadn't seen enough to tell.

"I just couldn't see enough even to guess," Wat answered. "It was dark on the upper stage, and I was still shaky from the blow when I saw him running out the gate."

"Did Elizabeth Brydges tell you anything about Essex's plans?"

"No."

"Which of the Admiral's Men have been meeting with Essex's people?"

"I don't know of any." Wat realized at once that this answer wouldn't work with Carlin.

"Try again. I think you recognized Singer and Towne when you left Elizabeth Brydges and followed them to the Mitre the night Slater was murdered. Am I right?"

Wat nodded. Then he thought he should tell Carlin about meeting Slater.

"I did follow them, but I didn't go inside. I don't think they killed Slater. I talked to Slater. It must have been just a little while before he was killed."

Wat told Carlin about following four men to the Mitre and being approached by Slater. "He was afraid and seemed to think I could help him. But I don't know how."

"What was he afraid of?"

"I don't know. He said he was a dead man."

"Did he say anything else?"

"Only something about papists and an actor being the one Tobye was looking for. I remembered that Topcliffe had asked me about someone named Thomas Southwell. He called him a papist scoundrel."

"You never told me about that. Did Topcliffe say any more about him?"

"He said he was the brother of a poet who was executed. And he said he had heard he was pretending to be an actor."

"Did Slater say what actor he was talking about?"

"He said he didn't know."

Carlin walked away, without waiting for any reaction from Wat. It seemed to him likely that either Singer or Towne or possibly Hearne was the player Tobye had identified, or perhaps that all of them had been acting for the Essex group. He now had a plan for identifying the killer. Somebody was already worried that Wat would remember something about the murderer. If word got around that Wat had remembered and was about to identify someone, the murderer might feel he had to act again. Wat would obviously be in danger; but if Carlin kept an eye on Wat and a close watch on Singer and Towne and Hearne, he should be able to spot the guilty person without much risk to Wat. He decided to try.

With a couple of his agents helping, he easily got people circulating word that Wat really knew who had killed Tobye. In the meantime he set out to find out more about Tom Hearne and his time on the continent. Henslowe had no detailed information about Hearne, but he doubted that he could have been with a company in Germany. Carlin went back to his records on his earlier cases, and on what was known about Topcliffe's earlier activities. Before he retired he had some new suspicions about the murders.

Wat was unaware of the rumors instigated by Carlin until he arrived at the theatre to get ready for another performance of *Jeronimo*, which continued through the summer to attract large audiences. John Pig came to him at once.

"What's this we hear about you identifying the man who killed Tobye?"

"What are you talking about?"

"Everybody's saying you've remembered who it was running out of the theatre that night. They say you're going to tell Carlin today."

"That's crazy. I don't know who was running away. That's what I told Carlin yesterday."

"Somebody thinks you know."

Several other players were collecting costumes and looking at lines, but they joined Pig to question Wat.

"Are you about to name one of us?" asked Towne. "Or was it someone from the Chamberlain's Men? I hope it was Kempe. He's been making a lot of noise lately."

"Where did you get this nonsense?" Wat protested. "I told Carlin yesterday I didn't recognize anybody."

"That's not what we hear," said John Singer. "And if you're going to identify somebody, you'd better do it quickly. Whoever is guilty may not want to wait to hear your news."

"This is silly. I don't know any more than any of you."

"Well, I hope whoever did it believes you," Singer said. "But I think you'd better watch your back."

Wat went off to pick up his costume for the Balthazar role, puzzled and worried. He didn't have any guess about how the rumor had started, unless Carlin had misunderstood him. And he wasn't sure that the other players had believed his denials. As he came back toward the stage, he heard someone call him, and he was surprised to see Captain Daglish. Daglish, Wat knew, was no lover of drama, and Wat had seldom seen him in the theatre.

"I heard the news, Wat," he said, "and I thought I'd better get over here fast. You're going to need a good blade around."

"What are you talking about?"

"You know well enough. If you know who's been swinging an axe around here, you can bet you're next on his list. That fool Slocum didn't catch a murderer. He was just talking big."

"But this is all a mistake. I don't know who's guilty. There's nothing I can tell."

"It won't hurt to be careful. I'm staying around until they arrest the varlet or I can get you home." The Captain loosened his sword and stood near the door where he could watch Wat.

Chapter Twenty One

❦

A Riot at the Rose

ANNE PAGE HAD REMAINED FIRM in her determination not to see Wat Gayton, although in a way his exploit with the lady in the coach had made him seem more interesting. She missed him and their walks together, but she still saw red when she remembered Elizabeth's condescension and arrogance. Perhaps she was more angry with Elizabeth than with Wat.

Both her mother and Joan Alleyn had noticed that Anne seemed more quiet than usual and that Wat had not been around the Mitre. Joan was concerned, and when she picked up the gossip that Wat could identify the murderer, she decided to speak to Anne. She found her helping her mother at the Mitre.

"Have you seen Wat today?" she asked, knowing quite well that she had not.

Anne simply shook her head.

"If you do, I think you ought to warn him. Around the theatre everybody is saying that Wat has remembered who it was who killed Tobye. They say he's going to tell Agent Carlin today."

"Is it true? Wat has always said that he couldn't tell who it was."

"I don't know whether he has remembered something or whether the whole thing is just gossip. Some are even saying that Wat's going to confess his own guilt. That's crazy, but I thought you would want to know."

Anne told herself that she wasn't interested in the affairs of Wat Gayton; but as soon as Joan left, she decided to walk over to the Rose just to see what was happening. She might find John Pig and find out whether Wat was really in trouble. By the time she got near the Rose, people were already gathering for the afternoon performance of *Jeronimo*, which remained one of the most popular of Alleyn's triumphs. Also, blocking Anne's way to the theatre, a large group of young men clustered along the river, moving toward the Rose, waving bottles and mugs and singing and shouting uncomplimentary comments about actors and the theatre.

Puritans and critics of the theatre like Richard Topcliffe charged that plays tempted apprentices to leave their work and dally in groups in taverns and playhouses. There was some basis for the accusation. For example, it had become a tradition for apprentices to desert their work on Shrove Tuesday and raid the stews on the Bankside, sometimes also disrupting performances at nearby theatres. Topcliffe and others like him were not above encouraging the apprentices, and frequently the apprentices were joined by rogues and vagabonds hoping for free ale or a share in any looting.

Anne was able to follow three or four theatre patrons who pushed their way past the rioters and headed for the main gate of the Rose. But just as she passed the last of the shouting apprentices, she felt a hand on her shoulder. Frightened she turned and recognized an old man she had seen in the tavern, the Richard Topcliffe who had threatened Wat with the rack. She pulled away and tried to run, but another man stepped in front of her.

"Just a minute, Mistress Page," Topcliffe said, "I need to talk with you."

Topcliffe, with his agents Fowler and Skevington, had been with the apprentices, encouraging them to invade the Rose and stop the performance. He had recognized Anne as she passed.

"I have nothing to talk to you about," Anne said. "Let me get on to the theatre."

"In good time," said Topcliffe. "But first I need to know what young Wat is up to. I hear he's about to name whoever has been murdering people in the Rose."

"I don't know anything about that."

"I think you do. We've seen you with Wat and that crew of sinners putting on plays, even young Pig who puts on women's clothes in defiance of the Scriptures. And I think you'll stay here with us until we find out what he's going to do. Skevington and Fowler stepped closer.

"Who's he going to name? I need to know."

"I don't know anything about it," Anne said and tried a step to walk away.

Skevington moved in front of her. "She's a pretty piece," he said. "Maybe we ought to take her home."

Topcliffe laughed.

In the theatre the audience for the afternoon performance was gathering early. Wat was already in his armor for the part of Balthazar, and John Pig was wearing the fine dress designed for Bel-imperia. They and other actors had heard the noise in the street.

"The apprentices are out," Pig said. "I saw some of them gathering when I was coming to the theatre. I think they're headed for the Rose."

"They must be thinking it's Shrove Tuesday," said Towne. "I'll bet somebody's been buying drinks for them. And they've probably picked up some rogues who are more trouble than apprentices.

Alleyn appeared; he had heard the noise. "Go call the watch, Johnny," he said forgetting that Pig was wearing a dress. "We may be able to turn them away."

Pig found Constable Slocum and two members of the watch already aware of what was happening, but not showing much disposition to interfere.

"They've been out all morning," Slocum said. "They got tired of causing trouble in the stews, and they seem to be headed for the theatre."

"Mr. Alleyn wants to see you," Pig said. He turned to run back to the theatre, and then he spotted Topcliffe and his henchmen outside the gate with a girl who looked like Anne. He went closer. It was Anne, and she seemed unable to get away. He ran back to tell Wat.

Slocum followed Pig to the stage. "Where's the rest of the watch?" Alleyn shouted. "Can't you do something about this?"

"We'll try to stop them at the gate," Slocum said. He moved toward the gate, but nobody thought the watch would have much effect.

Wat, as soon as he heard from Pig, moved down to the front of the stage, along with Captain Daglish, who didn't leave his side. He could see Topcliffe just outside the gate, apparently waving at some of the apprentices.

"I've got to go help Anne. He's probably heard the rumor that I know something and wants to use her to make me talk."

"I'm with you," said the Captain, with his hand on his rapier.

Wat in his stage armor, with a toy sword, and the Captain with his eye patch and his swagger made an interesting pair as they rushed out toward Topcliffe. Anne saw them as they approached and recognized the Captain, although she didn't know Wat in his strange costume until he spoke.

"Anne's coming with us," he said to Topcliffe. Anne tried to run to him, but Skevington held her arm.

Wat tried to pull Skevington away, and the Captain confronted Fowler, who had drawn his rapier to support Skevington.

Topcliffe laughed. "Oh, let her go with the boy in his soldier suit. We'll find out what we need to know. Put down your sword, old man," he turned to the Captain. "You might hurt yourself."

Anne rushed to Wat and threw her arms around him, in a strange metallic embrace. "Oh Wat," she said, "I'm so glad you're here. I was frightened." She looked back at Skevington and shuddered. Then she added, "I've missed you."

"Everything's all right now. I love you." It was the first time Wat had said it, but Anne didn't seem surprised.

The Captain sputtered a few words and made some gestures toward Topcliffe, but Wat pulled him away and they hurried toward the stage.

By the time they got there, the rioters had avoided the feeble efforts of the watch and were inside the theatre, moving through the pit. They pushed each other and moved erratically toward the stage, obviously with no purpose but to cause trouble. There were shouts—"A plague on all players" or "All players are rogues"— cries probably suggested by people like Topcliffe and not uttered very seriously. One of them had spotted Pig in his Bel-imperia costume and called out, "Look at that one in girl's clothes." Most of the audience either ran out of the theatre or made futile efforts to discourage the rush of the apprentices. Some of the groundlings joined the apprentices, to share in the excitement and perhaps have some free ale afterward.

By the time the rioters reached the stage, the theatre was in utter confusion. People shouting protests to the invaders or screaming in fear made more noise than the apprentices, who became preoccupied with trying to destroy any of the props for the afternoon performance that were on stage. One of them discovered the trapdoor in the middle of the stage and found his amusement in pushing some of his fellows down into the "hell" below the stage. They had no trouble pulling down the gallows prepared for the hanging in the play.

Slocum and the two other members of the watch retreated ahead of the apprentices and followed Wat and Anne and the Captain back toward the tiring house.

"We can stop them here," Slocum said, and took up a position with his halberd pointing to the confusion on the stage. He was joined by Captain Daglish with his rapier drawn and agent Will Carlin holding a pistol. Carlin was trying to keep an eye on Wat and also to watch the players he suspected of the murders. He saw Singer and Towne talking with John Pig, who was reporting on Wat's rescue of Anne. He could not find Thomas Hearne.

The apprentices had no focus for their efforts except the pleasures of vandalism; and by the time a few of them had forced their way to the tiring house door, most of the momentum for the raid was gone.

"Hold it right there," Slocum shouted. The Captain waved his rapier and Carlin flourished his pistol.

The apprentices stopped and backed away, although those behind kept shouting and pushing. And then they heard the sound of a shot. They turned in panic and ran quickly out into the court yard, thinking that Carlin had opened fire on them. It was not, however, Carlin's shot. There was a sound of someone running on the floor of the upper stage. Wat felt a sharp pain in his shoulder and fell back on the floor. Anne screamed and then knelt beside him. The Captain pulled back the armor that had deflected the bullet. The bullet had dug a furrow in his right shoulder but had not done serious damage.

"I'm all right," Wat said, "Go find whoever fired that shot."

The Captain left Wat with Anne, who had pulled off a scarf and was attempting to stop the bleeding from Wat's wound. He joined Carlin, who had rushed up the steps to the upper stage. They were too late. The upper stage was empty, but everybody could hear somebody running across the main stage; and then they recognized Tom Hearne, flourishing a pistol, and racing toward the main gate.

Slocum shouted "Stop, you're under arrest!" Carlin ran in pursuit, hampered by the apprentices, who tended to be on the side of anyone pursued by police.

But Topcliffe and Fowler and Skevington were still standing just outside the gate and were obviously interested in what was happening.

"Stop him," Topcliffe ordered. "He must be the murderer and the man we're after."

Fowler and Skevington waited on either side of the gate, and easily caught Hearne, who was exhausted from running and stopped without resistance.

"Who are you?" Topcliffe asked.

"It's you," Hearne almost whispered, suddenly looking delighted as he stared at Topcliffe. And without another word, and before

Fowler or Skevington realized what he was doing, he raised the pistol he was still carrying and shot Topcliffe in the face.

Skevington drew his sword, but Carlin arrived before he had a chance to use it on Hearne. Hearne, looking happy, handed the pistol to Carlin.

"I'm arresting you for murder and attempted murder as well as treason," Carlin said. "I think you're Tom Southwell."

Hearne didn't say anything.

"And you have to answer to me for wounding young Wat," Captain Daglish added.

"I'm sorry about Wat," Hearne said. "I have nothing against him. But I couldn't let him identify me before I finished what I had to do."

"And what is that?" Carlin asked. "I think I know."

"I thank you all for giving me the chance to finish today what I had to do. Topcliffe was the worst of the lot. They were all torturers and sadists, and I vowed when my brother was hanged they would pay for what they did to him. He was a fine poet and a man of God. And now I'm ready to die; I've completed my duty."

"Who are your confederates?" Carlin was still hoping he had uncovered a papist conspiracy.

"I needed no help but my memory of what happened to Robert. I've been planning for two years. I finally got back into the country and traced Timothy Rudd. He had posed as my brother's friend and then betrayed him for twenty pounds. He deserved what he got."

"But what about the others?" Towne asked.

"I found Tobye and Slater when I found Rudd. They were the spies who worked with old Topcliffe during the three years when he led the persecution of Robert. And they were still out looking for innocent victims. They thought there were papists in the theatre, especially among the Chamberlain's Men."

"Had they found any?" There was a voice from the tiring house door, and Will Kempe appeared.

"What are you doing here?" Alleyn asked.

"You always seem to turn up when there's been a murder," Carlin said. "What do you have to do with all this? Was Topcliffe after you?"

"I just came by to see how far Henslowe would go to get an audience. The apprentices just couldn't stand the idea of another showing of that old fustian of Tom Kyd."

"Get out of here Kempe," Alleyn said. "You have no business here."

"I don't know whether Tobye found anybody," Hearne continued, "but after I took care of Rudd, I decided to join the Admiral's Men. I had done some acting on the continent, and Henslowe needed players. I had no trouble then bringing Tobye and Slater to justice, although they both found out who I was."

"Why didn't you go back to the continent after you killed Slater?" Carlin asked.

"Topcliffe was still free. He was the one who enjoyed torturing people. I hadn't been able to get past his henchmen. But I had my chance today. I've finished what I had to do."

"Maybe what you did today was good," Singer ventured quietly, and there were some nods.

Slocum, enjoying his authority, moved to Hearne, or Southwell, and started to lead him off to prison."

"I enjoyed being an actor." Hearne said.

"You wasted your shot at Wat," Carlin said as Hearne was led out. "He couldn't identify anybody."

Carlin seemed not concerned that he had exposed Wat and been unable to protect him. He was pleased that he could take credit for solving the murders, although he was not uncovering a desperate plot against the Queen. He still had hope that he could find something subversive in the activities of the players who seemed to support Essex. He wondered why Will Kempe had turned up at the Rose, and was determined to find out.

There was some concern about the murder of Topcliffe in the Queen's Council, where a few members announced that the government needed to intensify its efforts to identify papists and other enemies of the Queen. Robert Cecil considered looking further into possible connections between the Chamberlain's Men and the Earl of Essex.

Alleyn had Wat, accompanied by Anne, taken to his house near the Rose, where a physician confirmed that his wound was not serious. Wat was taken to Mrs. Simpkin's later in the day, and Anne helped the widow nurse him until his recovery. Wat and Anne were happily in love, thinking about the future. Wat was dreaming about being another Edward Alleyn or even about writing plays. Anne was encouraging. Neither of them thought about Elizabeth Brydges.

Elizabeth Brydges was clearly out of favor at court, surviving only because of the protection of Essex. The Queen, moving toward the fortieth year of her reign, was increasingly impatient with her waiting women. She continued, however, to manipulate her courtiers skillfully, to manage the country's difficult relations with Spain, and to retain her popularity throughout the kingdom. In October there was another crisis in her relations with Essex. She gave Lord Admiral Howard an appointment as Earl of Nottingham, an office giving him precedence over Essex. Essex refused to attend Parliament or come to court. Again, Elizabeth relented and made Essex Earl Marshal, which gave him precedence over Howard, and all was well. But Essex was increasingly influenced by the flattery of his supporters, with his ambition driving him steadily toward disaster.

The Chamberlain's Men continued to flourish, with new plays by Shakespeare, including two parts of *Henry IV* and a number of revivals. The Admiral's Men had large houses at the Rose, as Henslowe acquired new plays and revived old favorites. Wat was busy, especially as Balthazar, as *Jeronimo* was repeated regularly during the fall. On the day of the apprentice's riot, however, the performance of *Jeronimo* was postponed, and that night one of the theatre cats dined on raw liver.

The Author

Robert Gorrell, educated at Indiana and Cornell Universities, is emeritus professor and academic vice-president at University of Nevada, Reno. He is the author of a dozen books, several in collaboration with the late Charlton Laird, and a variety of articles on Elizabethan drama, rhetoric, and the English language. Books include *Modern English Handbook* (7th edition, 1988), *English as Language* (1961), *Watch Your Language: The Mother Tongue and Her Wayward Children* (1994). His weekly newspaper column, *Straight Talk*, ran for a dozen years.

Colophon

Designed by Robert E. Blesse at the Black Rock Press, University of Nevada, Reno Library. The typefaces are Adobe Garamond for the text and JSL-Ancient and JSL-Blackletter for display. The typefaces on the cover are Scurlock and Celestia Antiqua. Printed and bound by Sheridan Books, Ann Arbor, Michigan.